MAIL ORDER MISSTEP

MAIL ORDER MIX-UP SERIES
BOOK 2

JENNIFER BRANSON

This is a work of fiction. Names, characters, organizations, places, events and incidents are either products of the author's imagination or are used fictitiously. Locale and public names are sometimes used for atmospheric purposes. Any resemblance to actual persons, living or dead, actual events, or actual locations is purely coincidental. All rights reserved.

No part of this book may be reproduced, or stored in a retrieval system, or transmitted in any form or by any means, electronic, mechanical, photocopying, recording, or otherwise, without express written permission of the author, except in the case of brief quotations embodied in critical reviews and certain other noncommercial uses permitted by copyright law.

Text and cover copyright © Jennifer Brandson 2023

Dedicated to:
My devoted readers
who love epic romances
with happy endings.
This series is for you.

CHAPTER ONE

Laurel, Mississippi 1885

"Listen here, girl, you'll do what I say," Elsie Jenkins' papa bellowed at her in a thick Southern accent, his round face bright red as the veins around his beady, brown eyes, and his thick neck bulged with rage. "I've put a roof over your head and food in your belly for nearly two decades now, and your marryin' Arthur Dorin is finally gonna put a little money back in my pocket."

"Papa, you can't mean to make me do it." Elsie pleaded as she pulled on the sleeve of her father's dingy cream shirt. "Mr. Dorin is an awful man. He beat his first wife before she died from consumption."

"Then you should learn from her mistakes, Elsie, and be a compliant wife. If you do what your husband says, he won't have a need to beat you." Her father yanked free and raised his fist in the air. "As it is, you're testin' my own patience with your whinin'. I have a good mind to show you what a sound beating is."

Elsie dropped her hand to her side and stumbled backward until she was flush against the rough wall of their small farmhouse, causing her red locks to bounce around her face. Shocked and frightened by his threat, she wrapped her arms around herself as if they were a shield. Her papa couldn't be described as a kind man, but neither had he ever proven to be a violent one. At least, she hadn't thought him to be, until she saw the menacing look in his eyes as he stomped towards her.

Her papa slammed his fist into the wall beside her face, causing her to flinch and look away. "You'll marry Arthur Dorin by week's end, or you'll be turned out from my home quicker than you can blink an eye. Do I make myself clear, Elsie?"

"Yes, Papa," she whispered, in her own soft

Southern accent, as tears filled the corners of her green eyes. "I understand."

"Good, that's a good girl." Her papa moved his hand over from the wall and patted the top of her head. "You don't need to show any of that stubbornness you got from your mother. By golly, it was the bane of my blight. I don't need you goin' and thinkin' you can act like her."

What Elsie wouldn't give for her mama to still be alive. Her Irish pride would've never stood for Elsie's papa selling Elsie off like a prized-cow. Her mama would've protected Elsie at all costs. But life wasn't fair, and Elsie had been without her mama for the past five years after she died in childbirth, along with her baby sister. Elsie had been left with only her selfish papa to take care of her. He demanded Elsie work her fingers to the bone and gave her little more than a passing thought until Arthur Dorin came sniffing around. She hadn't thought her situation could get any worse, but when Mr. Dorin offered to pay her father a windfall of money for her, she knew any chance at having a happy life was over.

"Now, go on and make supper before I change my mind about that beating."

Elsie scurried off towards the kitchen, pulling

out the items she needed to turn last night's dinner into a stew. She set to work filling the pot with water and placing it on the stove before cutting up the vegetables. Her hands continued on the task as her mind raced with thoughts of what she could do to escape Arthur Dorin's clutches.

She could tell from her father's resolve, it didn't matter how good she treated him or how hard she worked around the farm, he wanted the money more than he wanted her help. That meant she had to find another way out of the horrible situation.

Could she ask someone at the church for help? No, their pastor would tell her that it was her duty to obey her father. What about someone in town? Could she find a place to stay and work if her father kicked her out like he promised? No, they wouldn't want to get involved. What else could she do? Runaway? If she did, where would she go? How would she provide for herself? She doubted there were very many reputable options for a young woman, but it only took one. Tomorrow when she was in town picking up supplies, she would look through the newspaper. Silently, she sent up a prayer asking God to help her find a way out of the mess her papa put her in.

"How are you doing today, Miss Elsie?" Bonnie Trivail asked as Elsie entered the mercantile. "Are you here to pick up your weekly supplies?"

Elsie nodded. "Thank you, Miss Bonnie. I'd also like a copy of the newspaper."

The older brunette woman raised her eyebrows at the unusual request but handed one over without comment. Elsie collected the rest of her supplies, then hurried out of the store to the nearest bench. She didn't have long before her papa would become suspicious of her absence, and she would need every minute to form a plan of escape.

Elsie flipped open the paper to the 'help wanted' area. She skimmed through it, and just as she suspected, there wasn't a single job that a God-fearing woman would consider. What was she going to do? She couldn't stay in Laurel and marry Mr. Dorin, but what other choice did she have?

"What are you doing here, sitting all by yourself, Elsie?"

She glanced up and was relieved to see Sarah Johnson, her good friend from school. "I was just looking through the newspaper before I headed home."

"Why would you need to read anything in there?" Sarah inquired, her face scrunching up with disdain. "It's just gobs of bad news and dubious requests from strangers."

"Have you heard what my papa wants me to do?"

"Of course I have. Everyone else in town has too. I'm sorry that he's forcing you to marry Mr. Dorin." Sarah took a seat next to her friend on the bench. "I know you'd hoped for a better life than that."

"It's not that I don't want to get married. If it was to a kind and gentle man, I wouldn't object. Mr. Dorin, however, is a shrewd scoundrel. Who knew my father would turn me over to him for the right amount of money?"

"It doesn't seem fair that our lives are decided by the men in them, does it?" Sarah lamented. "My own father has decided that I'm to marry his business partner's son."

"At least Roger is a good man and will treat you fairly," Elsie pointed out. "Though I know you had your heart set on Lucas."

Lucas was the pastor's son and had attended school with all of them. He didn't have much in the way of means, which meant that Sarah's father didn't find him a suitable match for his daughter.

Sarah pressed her lips together as she squeezed her hands in her lap and shrugged with resignation. "What choice do we have?"

"I can't accept that being Mr. Dorin's second wife will be my future. There has to be something I can do about it."

"Besides running away and becoming a mail-order bride," Sarah teased with a giggle, "I don't see what choice you have."

"A mail-order bride," Elsie repeated. "Now, that isn't a bad idea."

"I wasn't serious, Elsie," Sarah rebuked. "You know those things are a scam, and half the time you arrive to find your groom is as ugly as a toad and twice as mean. You're better off with the devil you know, than agreeing to such a thing."

"You're wrong, Sarah. Sometimes those marriages do work out. My cousin has a loving, kind husband out West. She found him through an advert in the…" Elsie snapped her fingers as she recalled the name, *Matrimonial Times*—that's the name of the newspaper where the men place their requests." Glancing over at her friend, she requested in a hopeful tone, "Do you mind going into the mercantile and grabbing me a copy so my papa doesn't find out?"

Sarah's eyes grew round with bewilderment. "You can't be serious, Elsie. I don't want my own father thinking I'm planning on jilting my fiancé. You're going to have to find someone else to do your dirty work."

Out of the corner of her eye, Elsie noticed ten-year-old Billy Thudrow playing with a can and stick on the other side of Main Street. "Billy, do you mind coming over here for a minute? I need to ask you to do me a favor."

Billy scampered across the street, curiosity filling his eyes. "What kind of favor?"

"I need you to go into the mercantile and buy something for me."

"What do I get out of it?" he asked, as his eyes narrowed slightly in a calculating way.

"How about I give you enough to get a penny candy?"

"How about three?" Billy countered as he pushed out his hand with three fingers sticking straight up in the air.

"Two, and I won't tell your mama you pulled Linda's hair at church last Sunday," Elsie threatened with a sly smile.

Billy's eyebrows shot up in fright as he quickly nodded his head. "Two is fine. What you need me to buy for you, Miss Elsie?"

"It's a newspaper called the Matrimonial Times. It's right on the counter." Elsie handed over the money and waited as the boy scampered off to retrieve the requested item.

A few minutes later, he returned with the newspaper in his hands. He was sucking on a candy as he shoved the sheets of paper towards Elsie. "I told Miss Bonnie it was for my cousin who's stayin' with us. I figured you didn't want her to know it was for you."

"Thank you, Billy," Elsie said with a smile. She didn't like the fact the boy lied to cover up her deeds, but it did make it easier for her to keep her plans from her papa.

Elsie scanned the adverts, hope rising in her that maybe she didn't have to marry Mr. Dorin after all. "Let's see what other options are out there."

"I can't believe you're doing this, Elsie." Sarah shook her head, crossing her arms over her chest. "To be willing to leave Laurel to go out West to marry a complete stranger seems like such a wild and reckless idea."

"I'm desperate, Sarah. Mr. Dorin is not an

acceptable option, and my papa has left me with no other choice."

The first few men who placed adverts were not to her liking. They either were too old or requested odd qualifications, but the fifth one stopped her quick enough. She read it over and over. By the third time through it, she realized she might have found her way out from the rotten future her father had planned for her.

In immediate need of a strong, independent, young woman open to marrying a Pinkerton agent, requiring a steadfast, devoted wife. Must be willing to travel wherever the job demands, and keep the fire burning while away on assignments. Only a serious miss need apply via telegraph.

The wife of a Pinkerton agent? Could she agree to such a thing? She fit all of the man's requirements, and she could maintain a home the way he needed. "I have to go, Sarah. I'll talk to you later."

Elsie rushed across the street to the telegraph office. She pulled out the little bit of money she'd been secretly saving out of the supply money each week. Once she determined how much she could afford, she responded.

Resilient and capable at 19, ready to provide a refuge in the form of a home and commit to an agent in need.

"I'll check back tomorrow for an answer," Elsie explained to the telegraph operator. "I'd appreciate your discretion."

Luckily, the postmaster wasn't a fan of her papa after he sold his wife some chickens no longer capable of laying eggs. Elsie was rather certain he wouldn't go out of his way to tell him about her correspondence with the man out West.

When she returned home, she purposely hid one of the items to give herself an excuse to head back into town the following day. Hopefully, she would find the answer she needed to escape out West and leave her father and his despicable plans for her far behind.

Outskirts of Sioux Falls, 1885

. . .

Nolan Buckley glanced out the window of the train at the rambling Great Plains of North America. The sun was low in the late afternoon sky, kissing the top of the buttes that bestrode the train tracks that led deep into the Dakota Territory.

The pit of Nolan's stomach tightened with tension as he thought about meeting his new boss. When they hired and trained him to be an agent at the Denver office, he hadn't expected to have his first assignment to be so far away—or remote, for that matter. Nolan was a city man, born and raised in New York City, where he planned to spend his whole life. At least, up until the incident that destroyed his entire world. With one misunderstanding, his reputation was ruined over something he didn't do.

Before his situation could get worse, he made a quick escape. The money he took with him, however, ran out quicker than he suspected it would, leaving him with little choice but to find another way to survive. Since returning to New York wasn't an option, he decided to scour the newspapers for possible job opportunities. When he saw the advert looking for agents, he knew getting the job would probably fix all his problems. If he played his cards right, he could hide out using the various aliases provided by the agency. He planned on stashing away enough money from his job that within a year's time he could start over in Europe. No one would care about his past once he traveled halfway around the world.

Nolan arrived in Sioux Falls just as the final rays of the sun were fading out. After disembarking from the train, he meandered down the main street of town, stopping in front of the saloon. He debated whether he should grab a drink to calm his nerves before reporting for duty. Though it was tempting, he opted against it, knowing that if he arrived smelling of alcohol, it wouldn't be the best first impression. There would be plenty of time to drink after he checked-in at the office.

Reluctantly, Nolan continued down the street, surprised by how many businesses dotted both sides. He'd heard that the prairie settlement was large, but he'd had no idea that it was thriving enough to support dozens of establishments, especially out in the remote wild frontier.

Three doors further down, a wooden sign hung with the neatly painted words, "Pinkerton Agency." From the outside, the office was unassuming, but he supposed that was to be expected from an agency that prided itself on discretion.

Nolan ran his hands down his gray suit in an effort to smooth out the wrinkles, then pulled down the edge of his suit jacket, hoping he looked presentable. He pushed back his shoulders and lifted his chin as he entered the office. Once inside, he pulled off his hat, brushing his black hair off his forehead as he proceeded further into the building. He found a middle-aged brunette sitting behind a desk. She had her hair pinned up in a bun; eyeglasses sitting across the bridge of her nose. Her gaze moved from the file in her hands up to him. "Good evening, Mr. Buckley, We were expecting you much earlier in the day."

"My train ran late," he quickly explained, not liking that it sounded as if he was starting off on the wrong foot already. "I'm here to see Mr. Stansbury."

"*Agent* Stansbury," the brunette corrected with a frown. "Didn't they teach you how to address fellow agents while you were being trained in Denver?"

Nolan wanted to kick himself for the slip-up. He knew better, but after three long days on the train, he was exhausted. His mind had reverted to how he properly addressed people back in New York. "Of course, my apologies for the error. Is Agent Stansbury ready to see me?"

"I'll let him know you're here." The woman stood from her chair, her skirt shifting around her as she walked over to the nearby door, and poked her head inside. "Agent Stansbury, Agent Buckley is here to see you."

"Send him in," he heard his new boss order from the other side.

The woman turned around, gesturing for Nolan to come over. She pushed the door open for him to enter. "Good luck," she said in a way that made it clear she didn't have high hopes for him.

Agent Stansbury's dominating figure was sitting behind his desk, his hands clasped together in front of him. His chestnut hair was neatly slicked back over a strong, lean face, furrowed—no-doubt—from years of hard work. Nolan forced himself not to flinch under the other man's penetrating glare, made harsh by his stern brown eyes, buried deep within their sockets. "I suppose stopping just short of wasting my night after half my day is better than nothing." The senior agent pointed to the seat across from him. "Sit down, Agent Buckley."

Nolan did as he was ordered, knowing he needed his new boss to like him enough to give him the easy assignments. The last thing he wanted was to end up on some remote ranch tracking down cattle rustlers. "I'm eager to get to work, Agent Stansbury. Will I be working out of this office here with you?"

The other man shook his head. "Even though the town is growing daily, there aren't enough cases here in Sioux Falls to warrant that. We are the hub for the entire north central part of the country; however, which was why you were sent here. I have a case for you in the small town of Mitchell in the James River Valley."

"What's the case?" Nolan inquired, hoping that it would be a rather safe assignment. He wasn't one for risking his life for anyone or anything; he'd much rather investigate housekeepers for stolen silver or follow suspected cheating wives.

"You're going to be investigating the disappearance of items from a local train depot. Someone is stealing portions of mine deposits and shop owners' goods when they're coming off the train."

"I'm assuming you've arranged for me to have a job at the depot in Mitchell then?"

"I have," Agent Stansbury confirmed with a nod. "There are four suspects—all of whom have worked for the depot for various lengths of time.

They're a close-knit group, and don't take to outsiders well, which is why the agency is going to request you take on an additional part to your assigned alias."

Nolan stiffened in his seat, noticing that next to his own file was a secondary one. Did his boss expect him to work with a partner on this case? He hadn't planned on it, but if it was what was required, he didn't see how he could object.

"The men are married so you'll need a wife to help you gain access. They won't trust you if you come in as an unwed stranger."

"Wait, I'm confused," Nolan stammered out. "I don't have a wife."

"Not yet you don't, but I took it upon myself to place a mail-order advert once I determined the best way to conduct this investigation. She should be arriving tomorrow morning."

"You did what?" Nolan questioned much louder than he intended, his dark eyes widening with shock. "I didn't come here expecting to end up with a wife as part of my new alias."

"If you're unwilling to take on a wife, then I'm sure I can have another agent sent to take your place. I'd like to point out, however, that the agency has a proven success record with couples. If you do this, you'll be given assignments that no one else has access to."

Nolan could tell his boss wanted him to accept the conditions of the new assignment without any further resistance. Could he do it? Could he marry a complete stranger for his job? People had married for less noble reasons, and it wasn't as if he was duping the poor girl. She would know what she was getting herself into. Plus, there was always the prospect that at the end of the case, they could both decide it wasn't a good fit and annul the marriage.

"If you think this is what's best for the assignment, I'll do what you ask."

"Excellent." Agent Stansbury's face lit up with the first smile he'd cracked since Nolan entered his office. His boss handed him a small envelope. "There's enough money in there for incidentals for your travel and stay in Mitchell with your new wife. I've rented a house there for you, under your alias, as well as purchased a horse and wagon. Here is the file with your back story." He handed him a second, larger envelope. "I've also purchased two train tickets. You will leave tomorrow after your wedding. In the meantime, I've made arrangements for you to stay at the Crescent Hotel tonight." Nolan took the envelope and slipped it into the pocket of his jacket.

"Once your bride has arrived, bring her here so we can have the judge conduct the ceremony."

Nolan stood from his seat and exited the agency office. Rather than head to the hotel though, he made a straight line for the saloon. It seemed he was going to definitely need that drink after all.

CHAPTER TWO

As the train moved along the train tracks, Elsie watched the fields of farmland pass by. Even though the surrounding hills and trees were unlike the ones back in Mississippi, the endless rows of vegetables reminded Elsie of back home. She hadn't realized it would be as hard as it had been to leave Laurel behind. Despite how rotten her father became after her mother's death, she still missed him, not to mention her friends and church. Coming out West was supposed to be an adventure, but the farther she got away, the harder the trip became. Between the rough ride on the rails to the constant sea of strangers that came and went from the train, Elsie had never felt more alone.

Was this how she was to feel for the rest of her life—alone and disconnected? She had no expectations of love waiting for her in Sioux Falls, but she hoped for at least a friendship with her new husband. Would their lifestyle allow her room to make a new life for herself? Was it even possible to make friends and establish a home if she was constantly traveling? She reminded herself that she knew what she was signing up for when she agreed to marry a Pinkerton agent. Anything was better than marrying the tyrant her papa had planned for her, but she couldn't hope but dream of a life that was more than just being at her husband's beck and call.

"The Dakota territory is separated into two distinct areas, east and west of the Missouri River. The 'East River,' as it's called, is where we're headed," Anne Morris, a school teacher from New York City, was headed to the same place as Elsie to run the newly built school. The older woman had gotten on midway. She had taken it upon herself to mother and instruct Elsie along their journey, giving her a history lesson at each of their destinations. "Most of the population lives there because the land is fertile, giving newcomers plenty of opportunity for farming as well as hunting and fishing. The

'West River' is more desolate, and is predominately used for ranching."

"That's nice," Elsie mumbled out in an automatic response.

"Are you even listening to me, dear?"

Elsie turned her attention to the other woman. "I'm sorry. I was thinking about home."

"There's no point in dwelling in the past. Aren't you coming out here to start a new life? Best to focus on where we're headed, not where we've been. After my husband died, I didn't know what I was going to do, but then I figured I might as well put my education to use. Running the schoolhouse in Sioux Falls will give me a chance to make a life for myself now that Fred is gone."

"I'm glad you're so optimistic about what awaits us. I, on the other hand, face the possibility that I could end up in an even worse situation than I left behind. I've never even met my intended husband. Who knows what type of man he is," she lamented as a shiver of trepidation crawled up her spine.

"You mentioned he's a Pinkerton agent, correct?" Anne inquired. Elsie confirmed the information with a nod. "Then you shouldn't fret. I'm sure they do a thorough investigation before hiring a new agent. You should focus on all the positive things awaiting you. You're going to love Sioux Falls; it's supposed to be as modern as any city back East, and with all the same amenities."

Elsie didn't have the heart to tell Anne it didn't matter to her what Sioux Falls had to offer. She'd grown up with very little. Her papa wasn't the best provider, preferring to spend his time at the local bar and gambling hall. His selfishness only became worse after the death of her mama. He used the drink to console himself, choosing to squander away what little money they had in an effort to forget about his dead wife.

The train shuddered to a stop as the conductor announced their arrival. The passengers around her stood to their feet, gathering their belongings in a rush, before pushing towards the exit.

Anne climbed to her feet, pulling her own bag from under her seat. She gestured for Elsie to do the same. "It's time to start our new lives, dear."

There was no point in delaying the inevitable. Elsie did as the other woman suggested and retrieved her tapestry bag that contained her other dress as well as her skirt, two blouses, and a set of extra undergarments. She wore her only pair of boots—which were already wearing thin at the soles. Without the money to repair or replace them, she only prayed they would last through the winter. Besides her clothing, the only other items she brought with her was a single picture of her mama and her mama's wedding jewelry, which she'd managed to hide from her papa to keep him from gambling them away.

Elsie followed Anne through the car and climbed down the metal steps that led to the train depot's wooden platform. At the bottom, Anne turned to face her with a smile. "I suppose this is where our paths diverge. Of course, if you'll be staying in Sioux Falls, we'll be seeing each other around."

"I'm not sure where our first destination is going to be," Elsie admitted, her voice quivering from the fear of the unknown. Tears filled the corners of her eyes, prompting her to reach up and wipe them away, embarrassed that she was outwardly showing her distress.

"Oh dear, don't cry." Anne reached out and pulled Elsie into her arms. "It's going to be all right, you'll see."

"I do hope, that even if it's just for a short time, I'll stay here long enough that we can see each other again," Elsie mumbled into the other woman's shoulder. "I'm so scared of being alone."

"You won't be, dear, you're getting married. You may not realize it right now, but marriage is the greatest adventure you'll ever go on. Being married to my Fred was the best years of my life. I have the feeling that it's going to be the same with you and your new husband."

Elsie pulled back and smiled as a hiccup escaped her lips. She patted at her hair and tried to push the wrinkles from her simple blue day dress.

"I can't believe I'm crying right now. My fiancé is going to run the other way when he sees me looking like this."

"That can't possibly be true. You'll win him over with your charm and beauty the first moment he meets you."

The words were exactly what Elsie needed to hear. It comforted her to know that someone believed in her and that her situation was going to work out for the good.

A man started to wave, drawing Anne's attention across the platform. "That must be the mayor. He told me he would be here to meet me."

"Good luck," Elsie encouraged. As she watched the other woman walk away, she realized Anne had become a friend, and she would miss the other woman if her husband's job required her to move on from Sioux Falls.

A cold gust of wind slammed into Elsie, prompting her to slip on her coat and pull it snuggly around her. She wasn't used to the cold climate, and it sent an immediate chill through her body.

"Are you Elsie Jenkins?" a deep, masculine voice questioned from beside her, prompting her to jerk her head to the side.

Elsie was shocked as her green eyes discreetly inspected the man in front of her. She'd expected to be greeted by a rough-and-tumble cowboy, not a handsome gentleman in a refined suit. With his neatly coiffured black hair and chiseled face, she couldn't help but compare him to the man who worked at the bank back in Laurel. This was not the picture she had in her mind of a hardened detective who lived in the Wild West frontier. "Yes, I am. Are you the Pinkerton agent who placed the advert for a bride?"

"In a manner of speaking, yes. I'm Agent Nolan Buckley." He nodded his head slightly just before he scanned the area. "Do you have any other bags you need me to retrieve?"

She shook her head, lifting her single bag in her hand. "This is all I have in the world. I suppose it made my travel out here easier though—not much to worry about."

He tilted his head to the side as if contemplating her words. Without commenting on her statement, he turned and gestured towards the town behind him. "I'm supposed to bring you back to the Pinkerton office so that the judge can conduct the wedding ceremony."

"Right this instant?" she gasped out, her eyes rounding with apprehension. "Can I at least change my dress and freshen up? I've been in this outfit for over two days now."

Her eyes fell to her intended's own fancy attire. He wore a perfectly tailored jacket with a herringbone pattern which was repeated in the pants, giving the suit an affluent and graceful look. From the crisp, white shirt, to the sleek four-button vest over it, it was obvious he cared about appearances. This was only made clearer by his matching shoes, hat, and gloves which created the perfect balance to his outfit.

He pulled out his pocket watch and looked at the time. "I suppose we can stop off at my hotel room before we head over to the office."

"Hotel room? Are you only staying in Sioux Falls temporarily?"

"We both are. I have an assignment in Mitchell, which is about a day's travel from here. We'll be leaving in two hours on the final train, which is why we need to be married straight away."

Elsie nodded. As she walked beside the man she was about to devote her life to, she couldn't help but wonder about his character. Was he selfish and mean like her papa, or kind and generous like her mama? Would he be the sort of husband she dreamed of, or would he be the stuff of nightmares? Either way, it didn't matter now that she was here. She'd agreed to this arrangement, and she planned to follow through on her commitment. She just hoped she didn't live to regret it. Her life was never going to be the same again, and it was too late to turn back now.

Nolan paced back and forth in the hallway outside his hotel room, silently praying that he wouldn't regret what he was about to do. Inside, the woman he was about to marry was getting ready for their wedding. That was a sentence he never thought would apply to him. Nolan didn't consider himself the marrying sort. It wasn't that Elsie Jenkins wasn't pretty enough to keep his attention—because she absolutely was with her coppery red locks, gorgeous green eyes, and creamy complexion. The moment he saw her, he couldn't help but wonder what it would be like to wrap his arms around her petite frame and kiss her full lips. The issue was that he didn't have a monogamous bone in his body. He much preferred the option of enjoying the company of various women rather than just one. Could he really stand by this commitment and not stray? He wanted to be that man, but part of him worried that the first attractive woman that crossed his path would turn his head and cause him to forget his marriage vows. Of course, it wouldn't be the first time a beautiful woman got him into trouble.

"I think I'm ready," he heard Elsie say from the other side of the door. "Promise not to laugh. I don't have a wedding dress, so this is the best I could manage under the circumstances."

The door opened to reveal an unexpected sight. His future wife was standing in an elegant peach satin gown with a dainty square neckline that was trimmed with white lace. The dress's sleeves puffed out at the shoulders and flowed down until they gathered at the elbows. The waist of the gown tapered into a fitted bodice, adding to the elegance and grace. From the hips, the dress widened until it reached the floor. Her curls were gathered at the nape of her neck, exposing a set of gold and pearl earrings and a matching necklace.

"You look spectacular," he praised as he reached out his hand towards her. "It may not be a wedding gown, but it's every bit as pretty as any I've seen over the years."

"Been to a lot of weddings, have you?" she inquired with a quirk of her eyebrow as he helped her slip on her coat. She pinned her hat into place before letting him take her hand in his. "It would explain the fine suit you're wearing."

Nolan avoided telling her that back in New York he had left behind a wardrobe that rivaled any member of the royal family in Europe. When he fled, he only took a small fraction with him. As money grew tighter the longer he had to stay away, he ended up with less and less of his wardrobe. By the time he finally took this job with the agency, he had only two of his custom suits left. He quickly realized, however, that he was better off wearing clothes that blended in with the local farmers and miners out West than to draw attention to himself by looking like a dandy. He still couldn't bring himself to part with the last two suits, even though they had little purpose in his new life.

"I figured our wedding day constitutes as a special occasion." He placed her hand in the crook of his arm as he led her out of the hotel. "If you're wearing your best dress, shouldn't I give today the same consideration?"

Several people glanced their way as they walked down the street to the office. He knew they stood out in their far-too-fancy outfits for the middle of the day in the Dakota Territory, but he didn't care. Attention had never bothered him anyway, but he could tell from the way Elsie was acting, she was just the opposite. She pressed in against his frame, her head dipping low as she pulled down on her cream hat to shield her face from passing townsfolk.

"You shouldn't let anyone cause you to be bashful. You have every right to be excited about today. After all, it's not every day that a woman gets married."

Her eyes flashed up to meet his. "I've never done well with recognition. I'd much rather blend in with the scenery."

"I can't see how that would ever be possible, as pretty as you are." As soon as he said the words, he wished he could retract them. His observation seemed to only make her more uncomfortable, causing a flush to creep across her cheeks as she stiffened in his arms. "I'm sorry, you probably didn't want to hear that from me."

"It isn't that. Most women would want to hear that their intended husband finds them appealing; I'm just not used to receiving compliments."

"That's a shame. Perhaps over time, I can remedy that though by paying them to you often."

She laughed; the sound escaping from her plump lips sounding like the tinkling of tiny bells. "That's going to take some time getting used to."

"I'm sure it's not going to be the only thing—neither of us has been married before, so we'll just have to agree to give each other grace while we get used to one another."

"I can agree to that."

"We're here." Nolan signaled at the door to the Pinkerton Agency office. "Are you ready to go in there and get this done?"

She nodded as she squeezed his arm with her hand, her anxious eyes darting towards the door. "Even though my stomach is in knots and I feel like I might faint at any moment, I can't think of a reason not to do so."

"This is a big decision, Elsie. If you're having second thoughts, this is your chance to say so now."

"No, I'm all in—there's no going back for me. When I made the commitment to come out here and be your wife, I left my old life behind me."

Nolan knew what that was like. He'd done the same thing two years ago when he fled New York City. "Then it's settled. As soon as we walk through that door, we're starting our new lives together as husband and wife."

Elsie turned around, and for a moment he thought she might walk away. Instead, she moved towards the door and opened it. "Let's do this."

Inside the office, the same brunette secretary, along with Agent Stansbury and a man in a black suit—Nolan assumed was the judge—were waiting.

"Good, you got here on time." Agent Stansbury lowered his head towards Elsie. "Miss Jenkins, it's good to meet you. I hope your trip out West was amicable."

"I managed adequately, despite it being more grueling than I anticipated." Elsie removed her hat and jacket and placed them on the coat rack. "I'm just happy to finally arrive at my destination."

"*Temporary* destination," Agent Stansbury

corrected. "I assume Agent Buckley informed you about his assignment in Mitchell."

"He has, and I know we need to get this ceremony conducted quickly so we don't miss our train's departure. We can start right now."

Agent Stansbury grunted with approval. "I'm glad to see you're sensible about the situation. The last time I had an agent marry a bride, I had to spend a half-hour calming her down before she would go through with it."

"I wouldn't have come out West if I didn't think I could do this. Once I set my mind to something, it can't be shaken." Elsie turned to face Nolan, giving her hands to her soon-to-be husband as the judge took his spot in front of them.

Agent Stansbury and the secretary stood on either side of them, both there as witnesses to make the rite official. Both Nolan and Elsie repeated the words spoken by the judge, making vows to one another that he hadn't considered until they were being uttered out loud by the gray-haired man in front of him. "To have and to hold, for richer or poorer, in sickness and in health, for better or for worse, until death does part you." He'd thought he would have an exit hatch at the end of his assignment, but if Elsie didn't want to end the marriage once their assignment was done, could he be the one to do it? Could he go back on his word? If not, did that mean what he thought was a temporary solution to his problems, might end up being a permanent part of his life?

The ceremony moved so fast, and within a few short minutes, Nolan found himself sliding a gold band onto Elsie's finger just before the judged declared, "I now pronounce you, husband and wife."

Agent Stansbury placed a pen in his hand and directed Nolan to sign the marriage certificate. He watched as Elsie did the same, and it seemed surreal to see her name attached to his own. She was officially Mrs. Elsie Buckley now, a fact that had been abstract up until the moment the judge pronounced them husband and wife. For the first time in his life, he found himself responsible for another person, and he needed to take that veritable truth seriously, no matter how scary the prospect.

"Now that the two of you are married, you need to catch that train to Mitchell." Agent Stansbury ushered them towards the door. "The sooner you get the case solved, the sooner you can get back here for your next assignment."

Mutely, they walked down the street towards the

hotel to collect their belongings. As awkward as Nolan was feeling, he couldn't imagine how much worse this was for his new bride. He knew it wasn't the wedding she dreamed of. What woman in her right mind would prefer a quick, unemotional ceremony with no friends or family present to a traditional wedding filled with celebration and joy? A side-glance towards his wife confirmed his suspicions. There was no mistaking the sadness in her dejected demeanor. She was crying softly beside him, her shoulders shaking as she used the back of her hand to wipe at her tear-filled eyes.

"There's no need for that." Nolan pulled a handkerchief from his pocket and pushed it towards her. "I know it doesn't seem like it now, but our situation will get better."

"How do you know? By your own admission, you've never been married before." Elsie sniffed, as she used the edge of the satin square to dab away the wet streaks that marred her delicate cream skin. "What if we both fail miserably at it?"

"People get married every day. If it were that difficult to manage, you'd think word would get out and people would stop doing it." He hoped poking fun at their predicament might ease the tension. Instead, it had the opposite effect.

Her puffy, red eyes lifted up and glared at him. "I don't know what I was thinking. My mama taught me nothing good ever comes from making a rash decision. This was a huge mistake."

"I thought you understood what this was?" Nolan probed, confused by her reaction to their nuptials. She seemed fine before the ceremony, but since he slipped the ring on her finger, she'd steadily become more despondent over what transpired.

"I thought I did, too, but I'm scared of all the things that can go wrong. You could get hurt while working, my laugh could irritate you, one of us might snore. What happens when we realize this was a mistake but we have to stay married out of necessity? Over time, won't we end up resenting each other?"

"We don't have too," Nolan stated firmly. "We can agree to have this first assignment be a trial. If at the end of it, either of us wants out of the marriage, we can annul it. Would that make you feel better about the situation?"

Elsie bit her bottom lip as her brows furrowed together in contemplation. After a few moments, she slowly nodded. "I like that. Having a clear way out seems like the best option under the circumstances."

"Good, since that's settled, let's grab our belongings and head over to the train station. We don't want to miss our train to Mitchell."

A half-hour later, they were tucked away at the back of the train chugging out of Sioux Falls, headed further into the Dakota Territory.

Elsie turned towards her husband, giving him her undivided attention. "So, what's your assignment and why do you need a wife for it?"

Nolan debated about how much information to give his new wife. She hadn't been trained as an agent, but he didn't see a reason to keep anything from her. "I'm going to be investigating the disappearance of items from a local train depot. The suspects are all married, so a wife will not only provide me cover but help me gain access to their families."

"Earlier, when I questioned you about placing the advert for a bride, you didn't answer me directly. Your evasiveness makes me wonder if any of this was your idea."

Nolan was shocked by the astuteness of his new wife. Since he hadn't placed the advert, he never saw her response and knew nothing about her. Her uncanny ability to pick up on miniscule details could prove to be an asset rather than a mandated nuisance while working his case.

"Agent Stansbury was the one who placed the advert and picked you from the candidates who replied," Nolan confessed. "I wasn't keen on the idea when he told me, but I've planned to make do with the hand I've been dealt."

"Is that what you consider me? A bad gamble?" she accused, the hurt clearly reflected in her eyes.

"I didn't say that; I'm sure you'll do just fine playing the role of my wife," Nolan quickly corrected, worried she might start crying again, which was the last thing he needed. He didn't want to draw attention to them, considering that some of the other passengers might also be making their way to Mitchell. "In the meantime, why don't we try to rest a bit. It's been a long day." Nolan didn't wait for a response, but instead, leaned back against his seat, then tilted his hat over his face. He didn't know what else to say to Elsie to ease her apprehension, and it was better to be quiet than to say the wrong thing. Once they arrived in Mitchell, they could settle into their aliases and he could get to work on his case.

CHAPTER THREE

The deed was done. Elsie was now Mrs. Buckley. Just a few hours prior, she vowed to honor and support her new husband, and the ring on her finger was a reminder of that. She stared down at the gold band, wondering if she had made a mistake by marrying Nolan. Could she keep her vows and be the kind of wife he needed? It would mean significant time alone when he was on assignment without her, and when they were together, their identities would be constantly shifting to suit their latest case. Her life would never be ordinary again, and she wasn't sure how she felt about that.

The outside of the small, wooden rental house on the edge of Mitchell looked unkempt, with overgrown shrubs and trees. The thatched roof was low and hung over the front, with one chimney poking out at the center. Tiny, squared windows dotted both sides of the single door, which was covered in peeling paint.

As Elsie stepped through the threshold, she couldn't help but feel apprehension as she glanced around the sparsely furnished living room that flowed into the tiny nearby kitchen.

"I know it isn't much," Nolan excused, placing her bag and his own beside them in the entry. "But it was the only residence in town available. It was either this or staying above the saloon, which as a proper married couple, would draw negative attention we wouldn't want."

Elsie nodded, making a list in her head of what needed to be done to get the house in order. She welcomed the idea of throwing herself into a project that would have tangible results. Plus, it would keep her mind from thinking about living in close quarters with a man, a very handsome and virile man, that happened to be her husband. She pushed the troubling thoughts away, and let her fingertips drag through the dust on the kitchen table. "With a little bit of elbow grease, I can shine this place right up."

"I wouldn't bother."

"Isn't that my job?" she questioned with a quirk of her eyebrow and a wry smile. "Your job is to conduct the investigation discreetly while I provide you with a believable alias. What kind of a wife would I be if I couldn't at least play the part? What will people think if they came calling and the house looks untidy?"

"I think appearances are important when we're in town, but when we're in the privacy of our own home, we can stop pretending we're husband and wife."

Elsie couldn't help herself—she flinched; his cold description of their arrangement dug into her like pieces of broken glass. "I guess I didn't view it that way. I figured if anyone stopped by, we would want the house to give the proper impression. If you don't want me to do anything around here, then I suppose I can adjust to that." She flopped down on the couch, causing a giant puff of dust to spray up from the fabric. Instantly, she sneezed, but she couldn't stop at just one. A full baker's dozen came bursting from her, one right after the other until her chest ached from the rapid expulsions of air. At the end of them, her eyes widened as she glanced over at Nolan.

He let out a chuckle and shook his head. "Perhaps the house does need a little cleaning. You don't have to do it all by yourself though—I can help."

"Thank you for the offer, but after two trips on the train and our wedding ceremony, I'm exhausted. I can just take care of it by myself tomorrow."

"Are you hungry? I'm starving, and since we don't have any food here, we should probably grab a bite to eat at the café on Main Street."

She nodded as she stood to her feet and headed towards the door with Nolan by her side. "Supper sounds divine. Tomorrow, I'll pick up provisions at the mercantile after I finish fixing up the house."

They walked the short distance to the Waterside Café, a fitting name since the James River ran along the backside of Main Street. Mitchell was significantly smaller than Sioux Falls. As newcomers, they drew the attention of the residents that passed them by on the street.

"Good evening; welcome to the Waterside Café. I'm Lola Bryson. My husband, Terrance, and I own this place. He's in the back cooking, so you won't see much of him out here." Lola looked them up and down and nodded as if deciding she'd already made up her mind about them. "You must be new in town because I know everyone. What brings you out this way to the Dakotas?"

"We've just arrived in town this afternoon. I'm here for a position with the railway. I'll be working at the train depot loading cargo," Nolan explained. "This is my wife, Elsie, and I'm Nolan Winslow," he stated, using their fake last name.

"Pleased to meet you both," Lola stated with a warm smile. "We have a lot of people coming and going around here, so I wasn't sure if you were just passing through."

Elsie returned the smile, preparing to recite the story she'd practiced for hours so that it would sound natural. "That wouldn't be us. We hope to make a home for ourselves here in Mitchell. Coming from such a big place as Jackson, Mississippi, I've always dreamed of living in a small town. I can't wait to get to know everyone."

"Well, you've definitely come to the right place," Lola beamed with pride. "We're known for being the friendliest town in all of the Dakota Territory. You should make sure to come to church on Sunday. It's the best way to get to know the locals." She escorted them to a table towards the back. Once they took their seats, she handed each of them a menu with a list of selections from fish cakes to lamb stew. "I figure, if I seated you back here, you might not be bothered too much by other curious townsfolk. After a trip out here all the way from Mississippi, you must be exhausted."

"Thank you, we are indeed. It's nice to have a temporary reprieve before we get back to work settling into our new house," Elsie acknowledged.

"I'll leave you two for a bit so you can look over the menu."

"That won't be necessary. What would you suggest we order?" Nolan questioned, without looking at the menu. "As the owner, we can take your word as to what we should try first."

"We do have a special tonight; Terrance's baked salmon," Lola suggested. "He's known around these parts for it, so you can't go wrong with it."

"That sounds perfect," Nolan said, handing his menu back to the woman. "We'll take two, along with two lemonades."

Lola glanced between Nolan and Elsie but didn't comment on his decision to order for both of them. Elsie thought about objecting to Nolan's disregard for her preference, but then decided it would be better to deal with it privately than to chastise him in front of a stranger.

"I'll put the order in right away." Lola took

Elsie's menu with a sympathetic smile before turning around and scurrying off towards the kitchen.

"How do you know I like salmon?" Elsie probed, as she gently tapped the edge of the table with her fingertips, trying to keep herself calm.

"I just assumed you would be amicable to whatever the house specialty was," he explained in a tone that made it clear he didn't see a problem with what he did.

She'd had enough of men making decisions for her to last a lifetime—it was why she left home without a word to her papa. Elsie needed Nolan to understand that she wouldn't be a part of a marriage where her husband didn't view her as an equal. "I'm capable of making decisions for myself, Nolan. I didn't need you or want you, to order for me. I'd appreciate you treating me with more consideration than that in the future."

"I'm not sure why you're being so cross. I wasn't doing anything I haven't done a thousand times for women back in New York."

"I'm not most women," she seethed out in anger, barely managing to keep her voice to a whisper. "And if you can't even be bothered to let me order for myself, I don't see how this arrangement is going to work between us."

"I honestly didn't know that what I did would be a problem," Nolan protested, "but I'll make note of it and try to do better going forward. You have to remember, being married is as new to me as it is to you. I think we'll both have to give each other room to make mistakes and learn from them."

The tension in Elsie eased, grateful that he was willing to make the effort to put in the necessary work to make their situation acceptable for both of them. "Thank you, I appreciate you listening to me. It's more than my papa ever did."

"Was he a difficult man?" Nolan inquired, just as Lola returned and placed the glasses of lemonade on the table.

Elsie waited for the other woman to disappear before she answered her husband. "He was a harsh man, who cared only about himself. He planned to marry me off to a despicable monster for a handful of dollar bills. He thought it could fix the mess he made of our family farm after my mama's death. He was never the same after she passed. He only got meaner and more bitter with every passing day. I knew I had to get free from him before he took me down with him."

"I'm sorry for what your father tried to make you do, but I want you to know, I'm not that sort of man. I don't expect anything from you other than what you're willing to give to make our partnership work."

The last bit of apprehension fell away from Elsie as she let his kind words sink in. It wasn't often that a man didn't pressure a woman for more.

They spent the rest of the meal, as well as their walk home, discussing the plans for the house and what their next steps in the investigation would look like. By the time they were finished unpacking in their separate rooms, Elsie was confident that marrying Nolan had turned out to be the right decision. It might not be much in the way of a traditional marriage, but it was more than she hoped for when she set out to start her new life in the West.

"Well, I guess this is goodnight," Elsie said as she stood in the doorframe of the room across the hall from Nolan's.

"I suppose it is," Nolan agreed as he leaned against his own doorframe, staring at her with an inviting grin engraved on his face. "What possible reason could we have to stay up?"

Elsie's stomach tightened as she contemplated the look in his eyes. She could swear he was thinking about kissing her, and that unnerved her to no end. It wasn't as if the thought hadn't crossed her own mind once or twice since meeting him, but up until right now, she hadn't considered the possibility that the attraction was reciprocal.

Elsie wasn't sure what any of it meant, but it was definitely more than she had bargained for. She quickly stepped back and closed the door behind her, needing to distance herself from his penetrating blue eyes that had the possibility of seeing straight into her soul.

The next morning, Elsie got up early enough to see Nolan off for work. "I'm sorry there isn't anything I can use to make you breakfast."

"That's all right. I'll just get a bite to eat over at the café before heading to work."

"I promise to have it all sorted out by the time you get back tonight."

Once Nolan was out of the house, she set to work cleaning. It took nearly three hours and five buckets of water, not to mention a ton of scrubbing that left her arms throbbing from the pain. Once she was done, however, the house was sparkling from top-to-bottom and smelled of fresh lemons. As she glanced around the living area and kitchen, she couldn't help but be proud of how efficiently she polished the place into shape.

Next on her chore list was to make her way to the mercantile. Once there, she handed the list of items she wanted for the house. The store owner set to work gathering up the supplies, while Elsie moved around the room, looking at the different wares, which included cotton fabric of various shades and patterns, pots and pans, rifles and pistols along with ammunition, lanterns, and farming equipment, plus various other odds and ends needed for life out in the West.

Elsie must have not been paying close enough attention to her surroundings because she suddenly bumped into someone standing a few feet away. "Pardon me," she stammered out, her eyes flickering over to see who she'd so rudely bothered.

"That's all right," a pretty redheaded woman, who didn't look to be much older than her, excused her politely with a friendly smile. "Are you new in town? I don't think I've ever seen you around, though I'm not in town all that often myself. My family doesn't live in Mitchell directly, but on our family farm just to the east."

"I grew up on a farm back East," Elsie blurted out, then remembered that wasn't part of her backstory for her alias. It wasn't a huge mistake, since she hadn't told anyone about her past, but that meant she would have to keep that detail of her past true going forward. "I'm Elsie Winslow; I just moved to town with my husband, who got a job working at the train depot."

"It's nice to meet you, Elsie. I'm Cara Cassidy."

"Pleased to meet you," Elsie stated in return. "It's heart-warming to find a fellow Irish woman all the way out here in the Dakota Territory."

Three children burst into the mercantile, all rushing towards them. The two younger ones, a boy and a girl, pulled on Cara's skirt begging for penny candy, while the oldest girl stopped just to the side of them. "I told them we should wait at the wagon, but they didn't want to listen to me, Ma."

"That's all right, I know you tried your best, Susan." Cara reached out and ruffled the hair of the boy while patting the girl on the back.

"I can't believe you have all these children, and with such varying ages. You don't look nearly old enough," Elsie observed.

"Oh, I didn't give birth to them," Cara explained as she looked over at Elsie. "Though that doesn't make them any less mine. I loved each of them from the moment I married their pa a few months back."

"You're the best Ma ever," the little boy exclaimed. "Especially if you buy me a piece of candy."

"I want one, too," the little girl whined beside him.

"I suppose one piece each won't spoil your appetites before lunch," Cara relented. "Both of you may go pick one out. You can get one too, Susan, if you wish."

The children moved across the room over to the counter where the candy was located.

"It seems you have your hands full."

"I do, but I wouldn't trade it for the world. I love my life, and when I answered my husband's advert in the newspaper, I never knew it would lead to me being so happy."

"You're a mail-order bride, too?" Elsie asked with shock. She hadn't expected to find someone who had made the same bold decision to leave their life behind and move out West to marry a stranger. "I'm from Mississippi but my husband's from Colorado."

"It's quite common out here, considering

women aren't plentiful. A lot of lonely frontier men want a wife, and they're willing to place an advert to find one."

"It's nice to know I'm not alone."

Cara reached over and squeezed Elsie's hand. "Of course not; I know we've just met, but I can see already, we're going to be fast friends."

"I'd like that."

"Good, which means we'll have to get together for lunch sometime in the near future. Maybe we can do so the next time I'm in town. In the meantime, will you be at church on Sunday?"

"I will," Elsie confirmed.

"Good, then you and your husband will have to sit with my family," Cara offered.

Elsie wasn't sure how being friends with Cara would benefit Nolan's case, but she also didn't see how it could hurt it. If they were to assimilate into the town and make friends, it would help solidify their aliases. Wouldn't that be the right thing to do?

"Thank you for the offer. That would be lovely."

Elsie finished up at the mercantile, picked up some items at the butcher shop and grocer, then made her way home. Once she put everything away, she set to work making supper for Nolan. She fried up the pork chops and boiled and mashed the potatoes, before making a pan of gravy. Her final project was to make a batch of molasses cookies, before setting the table for the evening meal.

"That might be the best smell in the world," Nolan praised as he came into the house. "I figured I would find a hot-cooked meal when I got home, but I had no idea I was going to find something as amazing as this." He glanced around the house, and added, "And the house; I had no idea that it was possible to make such a small, simple place feel so welcoming. You've truly outdone yourself, Elsie."

"Thank you," she muttered softly, her cheeks blushing from the blatant praise.

"Don't tell me no one has ever told you what a wonderful homemaker you are?" Nolan inquired with surprise. "Your mother must have taught you well."

"She did," Elsie admitted, trying to keep the pang of sadness over her loss from bubbling up and ruining the moment. "Everything that was ever good in my life, I owe to her."

"Well, I think she would be proud of all you've accomplished around here in just one day. It speaks to how hard of a worker you are."

Elsie gestured for him to take a seat at the small

kitchen table, then took a seat across from him. The food was already on the table, along with the simple place settings that came with the house.

"I hope you enjoy what I made, but be warned, it's nothing as fancy as what I bet you ate in New York City. Our meals back home consisted of the crops we grew in the fields and the animals we raised on the farm."

Nolan scooped some of the potatoes onto his plate before grabbing the closest pork chop. "I'm sure the food will taste delicious. I found over the years, more often than not, the more elaborate the meal looks, the less I like what's hidden under all the dressing. Give me a well-cooked piece of meat and a side of potatoes any time."

"I'm glad to hear that you don't expect me to cook like those fancy chefs I saw through the windows of the restaurants in Jackson. I remember walking down the street with my mama, and wondering what it would be like to eat in a place like that."

"You've never eaten in one before?" Nolan inquired, with a raise of his eyebrows.

Elsie shook her head as she placed food on her own plate. "My papa would have skinned us alive if we ever even thought about it. We didn't even eat at the café in Laurel, let alone a fancy restaurant in the city. My mama was a pretty great cook though, and she was in the middle of teaching me before she passed away. I learned the basics, but I never got the finer parts down." She reached her hands across the table and curled them in a way to make it clear she wanted him to take them. "Do you mind praying over the meal before we eat?"

"Not at all." Nolan took her hands in his, causing a warm tingling sensation to crawl up both of her arms. Her eyes met his, and she could tell from the look in them, he felt the connection, too. Neither of them addressed it as Nolan prayed. "Lord, we thank you for this day, and the food you've provided for us. We ask that you bless it to our bodies, allowing it to nourish us and prepare us for the work we have ahead of us. In Jesus' name, we pray, Amen."

"I appreciate you doing that," she whispered across the table, as she took her hands back, missing the warmth the moment they were no longer nestled in her husband's. "Dig in."

It took only a single bite for Nolan's eyes to widen with admiration. After he chewed and swallowed it, he stopped just long enough to sing her praises. "You were far too humble about your cooking abilities. Any husband would be proud to have you cook for him."

"Thank you." She could feel her cheeks flush from the compliment as she took a sip from her cup of the fresh lemonade she had made earlier in the afternoon. "It's kind of you to say so."

"I mean it; your food is as good as any I've ever tasted in the finest restaurants in all of New York."

"I've been meaning to ask you about that; from your fine clothes to your refined pallet, you don't seem the sort to find yourself working as a Pinkerton agent, let alone out West. How did you end up taking this job?"

"An incident happened back home, and it was easier to leave than to stay and suffer for something I didn't do. The first year I was gone, I had enough money to sustain me. When I realized my temporary absence was turning into a permanent one, I knew I had to find some way to support myself. I saw the advert in the newspaper and decided it was better than most of the other options out there."

Elsie was certain there was more to the story than he was telling her, but pressing her new husband about the matter wouldn't win her any favor. She hoped in time, he would trust her enough to open up and tell her the details of why he left New York. Until then, she would be grateful for what he was willing to share with her. "It seems we both left behind some unpleasantness in our past."

"And now, we have the chance to start over together. I'll have to thank Agent Stansbury for doing such a good job when he picked you out as my wife. From the way things look around here, it's clear you know how to properly run a household."

"My mama wanted me to be a good wife when it was time to marry. She started training me early to make sure I was ready. I remember doing chores around the house as young as five years old. This was nothing." She gestured around the house, then picked up the pitcher of lemonade and refilled his cup. "That's enough about my day though; I want to know about yours. What happened when you got to the depot? Did you notice anyone that seemed suspicious?"

"Wouldn't that have been nice?" Nolan mused. "Unfortunately no, everyone seemed calm and collected. They were cordial, but I wouldn't describe them as friendly. I have a bad feeling it's going to take more time than I anticipated to get them to trust me."

"I have confidence in your training. I think

you'll be able to crack this case sooner than you think."

"God willing, I hope you're right."

"We need to discuss our plan for church today."

"Our plan?" Nolan asked with confusion. "I thought the purpose of going was to keep up appearances and solidify our story."

"Well, since the men are proving more guarded, perhaps I can find a way to get their wives to trust me. Isn't that why I'm here?" she countered, as they walked down Main Street.

"I was under the impression that you were here to solidify my alias, nothing more."

"Why limit my role in all this when I can do more than be just a wife? Think of it this way, the quicker you wrap up your first case, the more you will impress Agent Stansbury. If you do well, you'll get an even bigger case for your next assignment and that will be good for both of us. The more you succeed, the more it helps me, too."

Nolan knew she had a point. Her future rode on the success of this case as much as his did. If he was to continue on as a Pinkerton agent, he needed to prove himself capable on this case. He wasn't sure he was willing to risk someone else's life, however, let alone the woman he promised he would protect. "I don't know how I feel about you getting involved in the case."

"Then why did you tell me about the case on the train ride here? Surely, that wasn't necessary if all I was to be was part of your fake identity. By telling me, you must have wanted my input."

His wife was like a dog with a bone. No matter how hard he tried to persuade her to stay clear of the case, she seemed bound and determined to get involved. "What if something goes wrong and you're put in jeopardy? I wouldn't want any harm to come to you."

"I don't have to do anything other than gather information from the wives. It poses no threat to me," she assured him. "I promise, I'll be safe."

Nolan could tell no matter what he said, Elsie was going to make sure she was involved with the case. It would be better for both of them if he directed her engagement with the suspect's wives, rather than let her go it alone without oversight. "I suppose if you were to ask a few questions in a discreet manner—once you've established friendships with the wives—that wouldn't be the worst idea. Today, just focus on getting the other women to like you."

They arrived at the white, wooden building at the edge of town and made their way up the steps. Several people introduced themselves with welcoming smiles as they entered and took seats towards the back of the modestly small room filled with half a dozen oak pews split by an aisle. A matching pulpit made from the same lumber sat at the center of the aisle with a wooden cross on the wall behind it.

"I'm glad to see you made it," a friendly redheaded woman beamed as she came up to them with a tall, thick man with brown hair and matching eyes. They were followed by three children; none of them looked like the mother.

"I insisted that we come, even though we're still recuperating from our long trip out here." Elsie gestured to Nolan beside her. "This is my husband, Mr. Nolan Winslow. Nolan, this is Mrs. Cara Cassidy—we met at the mercantile the other day."

Nolan was surprised that his wife hadn't mentioned meeting the other woman, but masked his reaction. It was as much his fault as it was hers since he wasn't in the habit of asking her about her day. Maybe if he had, she would have told him. He needed to learn to be better about that.

"Pleased to meet you, ma'am," Nolan greeted with a slight nod of the head.

"Likewise," she returned. "This is my husband, James Cassidy, and our three children, Susan, our oldest, Becky, our middle child, and Thomas, our youngest."

Each of the children greeted them, as did James.

"Why don't you sit with us," James offered, as he gestured to a pew towards the back of the church. "It's never easy being new in a strange place."

"Thank you for the offer," Nolan replied, taking a seat far enough down the pew that there was enough room for his wife and the Cassidy family.

The service passed by quickly with the pastor speaking about how God is the everlasting vine. Nolan had attended a church back in New York, but it had been more for social and business reasons rather than to actually hear the message from the clergy. As he listened to the sermon now, he found himself captivated by the analogy that every believer was an extension of the vine by way of being a branch, and that by maintaining a relationship with God, each believer would produce fruit. Without God, a person would wither and be useless. Nolan had never thought about God like that and found himself excited about his new church.

"We have to be getting back to the farm, but how about next Sunday we go out to lunch after service?" Cara offered. "Before we leave though, I want to invite you to the women's auxiliary meeting this coming Friday here at the church. We're going to be planning a pie auction to raise money for the town's first schoolhouse we want to build. Right now, school is held here in the church, but it's not big enough anymore. The children really need a place of their own."

"What a noble cause; I'd love to come and help support. I can even share my secret crust recipe. I won two county blue ribbons for my pie."

Nolan glanced over at his wife, intrigued by every new detail he found about her. He had no idea that he was married to an award-winning baker. He'd have to ask her about that at a later time when they were alone. It seemed the sort of thing a man should know about his wife, and he didn't want anyone questioning why he didn't.

"That would be wonderful. I look forward to spending more time with you Friday evening." Cara ushered her family out of the church, leaving Nolan alone with Elsie.

"Let's take our time leaving," Nolan whispered to his wife as they stood from the pew. "The workers from the depot and their families are sitting towards the front."

Elsie pretended to be looking for something in her tapestry bag, giving them an excuse to stay behind. Nolan watched from under hooded eyes, hoping that they would see them and stop to talk with them. After a few minutes, the group made their way down the aisle. Most of the members passed by, and Nolan had nearly given up hope they would notice them, when the second to last worker, John Straits, stopped and shouted to the rest. "Look here, it's Nolan Winslow."

The rest of the group turned around and faced Elsie and Nolan.

"Well, isn't this a surprise? I thought you'd be home enjoying newly wedded life," David Buckson jested, looking from Nolan to Elsie. "Church is what you settle into doing after a couple of years of marriage and have tired of one another."

"Oh hush now, David," a middle-aged woman with graying brown hair said beside him. "Don't scare them away." She smiled at both of them.

"Forgive my husband, he's under the mistaken impression that he's humorous. I, for one, am glad to see new people here. I'm Julia Buckson—pleased to meet you."

"It's nice to meet you, too," Elsie returned the smile with a small nod.

"Let me make introductions," Julia continued. "John Straits is the one who noticed you. His wife is Barbara. On the far end, you have Matt and Georgia Boggs. Next to them, is Timothy and Dina Stone."

Nolan repeated the names in his head, tying the wives to the men from the depot. He hoped that Elsie was doing the same.

"So, what do you think of our little town?" Barbara, the youngest and prettiest of the women, with dark black hair and eyes, asked with a friendly smile. "Mitchell is a great place to raise a family, or at least, that's what the other women tell me. I won't know for a couple of more months." Barbara patted her overly round belly with affection, making it obvious she was pregnant.

"We're just over-the-moon excited to start our new lives as newlyweds in such a sweet town," Elsie gushed, the practiced made-up story rolling off her tongue as easy as butter on warm bread. "We've only been here a couple of days, and we already feel like we're home."

"I wouldn't get used to it," Dina snapped out. "People find the West to be far more unforgiving than they ever predicted. I doubt you'll last long out here." She was the oldest of the women with silver hair and cold blue eyes. As she looked around the group, she made eye contact with each of the other women in a way that made it clear, she was in charge. "Ladies and gentlemen, we have plans for lunch, and should be on our way."

As they shuffled out of the room, Barbara gave a sympathetic look back, as did a couple of the men, who seemed to be saying sorry with their eyes, though they didn't say it out loud, most likely from fear of being rebuked by Dina Stone.

"You're right, they're more guarded than I anticipated," Elsie confessed with a frustrated tone as they headed back to their house. "It's going to take some work to get them to let us into their group."

"At least now we know what we're up against. It's going to take us working together to find a way to get at the truth about who is behind the theft."

CHAPTER FOUR

Elsie spent the next couple of days thinking of ways she could get to know the other women. She then remembered Cara Cassidy had invited her to the women's auxiliary meeting. She realized she had the perfect opportunity to be around the other women, and hopefully find a way to befriend them.

She arrived at the church with a homemade cherry pie in her hands, hoping that the offering would make her path to friendship easier. When she walked inside, however, she wasn't so sure her plan had any chance of working when she saw the wives of the depot workers. The only one smiling at her was Barbara, and she seemed to only do it when the other women weren't watching her.

Elsie glanced around the room, hoping to find Cara, but she wasn't there. Did that mean her only friend in town wasn't coming? Should Elsie stay anyway?

"I don't think we've been introduced." A middle-aged brunette with bright green eyes came up to Elsie. "I'm Lydia Breckinridge, and my husband is the pastor of the church here in Mitchell."

"It's nice to meet you. I'm Elsie Winslow," Elsie said in return, noticing that the other woman seemed unaffected by the veiled hostility she was receiving from the other women in the room.

Elsie suspected it was Dina's doing. The older woman didn't like her from the get-go, and it would make sense that she would turn the other women against her to keep Elsie from joining their group. It just meant that she was going to have to work twice as hard to get them to like her.

"How did you find out about the auxiliary meeting?" Lydia asked with curiosity.

"Mrs. Cassidy invited me," Elsie explained. "I brought this pie for everyone to try."

"I'm not sure why you thought that would be necessary," Dina snapped out, her eyes narrowing into slits as she glared at Elsie. "This isn't the actual event, just the planning for it."

"Now, now, Dina, there's no reason to be testy," Lydia kindly rebuked. "Mrs. Winslow is here to volunteer her time just like the rest of us. We should welcome her desire to want to help others. After all, it's an attribute that we all admire and strive for in our own lives."

Dina let out a small "humph" under her breath and turned to walk away, gesturing with her head to the other women. They didn't hesitate, following her lead without pause.

"Don't mind them, Mrs. Winslow. Dina likes to think she's in charge, and everyone else just lets her. You're more than welcome to sit next to me during the meeting. There are a few other women who should be showing up, and you'll find they are much more agreeable than Dina and her friends."

Even though Lydia thought she was comforting Elsie, what she didn't know was that it didn't matter if all of the rest of the women in town liked her. If the train depot worker's wives didn't accept her, she wouldn't be able to help her husband with his case. She wanted to prove herself more valuable than just a simple homemaker. She wanted him to see her as an equal, capable of doing more than he thought possible.

"Why don't you set your pie down on the table over there while I grab some plates and forks from the back office," Lydia suggested, pointing to a small table on the east side of the church before moving off in the opposite direction.

Elsie walked the short distance to the table and placed her pie down. "That looks delicious," Cara raved, as she came up beside Elsie. "I can't wait to taste an award-winning pie."

"You can't be serious? How could you possibly win? It is the most common pie I've ever seen." Dina asked in a mocking tone, as she stomped over to them with her hands on her hips.

"She won *two* blue ribbons for her pies back in Mississippi," Cara defended. "She brought the pie here so we could taste it. She even offered to share her secret crust recipe."

"We don't need her pie or her recipe," Dina seethed out in anger. "Everyone knows my pie is the best in town. It will easily fetch the highest price at the auction."

"Of course it will, Dina," Georgia soothed from beside her friend with her thick Southern accent.

"Everyone knows your apple pie is the best in all the Dakotas."

Elsie wanted to say something to make the other woman stop from verbally attacking her, but she didn't know what that would be. She couldn't very well deny her pies won ribbons when they did, but she could assure the other women she didn't plan to compete against them for anything. "Dina, I don't—"

"Mrs. Stone," she corrected with a glare. "We aren't acquainted well enough to be addressing each other by our Christian names, nor do I think we ever will be."

"My apologies, Mrs. Stone," Elsie quickly amended. "As I was saying, I don't have any plans of competing against you, or anyone else for that matter, when it comes to making pies. I simply wanted to help raise the money needed for the new schoolhouse. If that's going to cause more problems than solve, I can forgo providing a pie for the auction."

"That won't be necessary," Lydia stated as she came up to the group. "Everyone is welcome at these meetings, and are encouraged to help at the different functions. We happily accept any contributions you are willing to give, Mrs. Winslow." She placed the plates down on the table and then set to work cutting small pieces for all the women. She handed them out and gave them each a look that made it clear she wouldn't accept anyone passing up the chance to try it.

Obligingly, each of the women took a dainty bite, the last one being Dina. The other women's eyes rounded with surprise, but none of them commented except Julia, who couldn't help herself as she blurted out, "This has to be the best cherry pie I've ever tasted. The crust is so flaky—I didn't even know it was possible to make such a lush crust."

Dina slammed her plate down on the table, frustration visible in every wrinkle of her furrowed face. "I've had my fill of cherries to last a lifetime. We should start the meeting."

"Don't fret, Dina, your pie is every bit as good as hers," Georgia consoled her friend. "I'm sure Julia thinks the same thing, right?"

Julia nodded her head vigorously. "Of course, no one's pie compares to yours, Dina." She was obviously trying to make up for her outburst.

Dina spun around and stomped off towards the

area set up with chairs for the meeting, with the other two women chasing after her.

"No one wants to admit it out loud, but your pie's better," Barbara whispered with a secretive wink before scurrying off after them.

"She's right," Lydia agreed, "but I shouldn't say that since I'm the pastor's wife. I see the rest of the women arriving, so I need to go greet them."

Once they were alone, Cara leaned towards her friend with a sympathetic smile. "Don't take anything Dina does to heart. She's always like that with new people. It took her months to accept I wasn't just passing through town. I'm still not even sure if she likes me."

Elsie didn't have months, or at least, didn't think Agent Stansbury would appreciate it if it took that long to get to the bottom of the depot theft. She needed to figure out a way to earn the trust of the train depot workers' wives, or she'd end up proving Nolan right that her only value was as a homemaker. Elsie refused to let that happen. She wanted to be more than that, not only for her husband but for herself, too.

All week long, Nolan was blocked at every turn when he tried to make progress in his investigation. Every time he thought he might have a chance to look for clues in the train depot office, someone would come inside and interrupt him. It almost felt like it was intentional—as if because he was the new guy, they didn't trust him alone in the office. He would have been offended if their suspicions didn't have a level of validity. After all, he was there to spy on them and figure out which one of them was stealing.

"I wish my wife would pack me something other than a hard-boiled egg and a hunk of old cheese for lunch," John complained.

"Welcome to life after a couple of years of marriage," David teased. "This is what you have to look forward to after newly wedded bliss wears off, Nolan. New wives go out of their way to make you happy, but as the novelty of marriage expires, they go from making delicious meals to sending you whatever they scrounge up."

Nolan inspected his own tin container, noting that Elsie had indeed sent nearly the entire contents of their kitchen. Between the meatloaf sandwich, boiled potato, fresh apple, molasses cookies, and tin jug of lemonade, Nolan had a feast fit for a king.

John leaned over and glanced in Nolan's lunch tin. "Yep, his wife is still trying to impress him. I guess I need to accept that my charisma isn't working on Barbara like it did once."

"Stop your complaining," Timothy barked out in frustration as he frowned at the other man sitting across from him at the table in the depot office. "You're always grumbling about something, John."

"Besides, it's about time we get back to work," Timothy ordered. As the manager, he was always serious and wanting the rest of the workers to concentrate on getting their jobs done quickly and efficiently. "We've taken enough time off for lunch."

The men did as their boss told them, gathering up their lunch supplies and putting them away before standing up to head back to the depot.

"I need to visit the latrine before getting back to work," Nolan stated, allowing the other men to exit the office and head toward the cargo hold as he set off in the other direction. He let a couple of minutes pass before turning around and heading back to the office.

Once he was sure no one was around, he slipped inside and started going through the desk and file cabinets. He didn't find anything out of the ordinary, but he did come across the schedules from the past couple of months. He pulled out his own notepad from his pocket and glanced at the dates he had written down for days when items went missing from the depot. There was no possible way Matt or David could be involved, which only left John and Timothy as possibilities.

As the manager of the depot, Timothy would be more able to cover up his trail, which made him seem more likely to be the culprit, but he didn't want to rule John out either. He would just have to make an effort to get to know both men, and perhaps, get Elsie to try to do the same with the women It might be harder with Timothy's wife, since Dina Stone hadn't taken a liking to Elsie. That also made him suspicious because if Timothy's wife knew about his theft; it would explain why she was guarded against strangers.

Nolan slipped out of the office and headed to the cargo hold. He helped the men finish up the last of the chores, then swept out the area with the help of John.

"You should come out with us to the saloon after work," John offered with a grin. "That is, if the missus will let you."

"My wife doesn't run me," Nolan stated

candidly. "I do what I want, when I want. Marriage hasn't and won't change that."

"Don't let your wife hear you say that," Matt jested with a chuckle. "She'll make sure you sleep with the dogs if you do."

"Speaking from experience, Matt?" David teased with a wry grin. "I hear you get put out with the dogs more often than you end up in your own bed."

"I'd be offended by that if I didn't love my dogs nearly as much as my wife," Matt countered.

"Men, that's enough. Put the jokes aside until after we're finished for the day," Timothy ordered with a scowl. "We need to make sure everything is ready for the night shift."

The workers finished the last of their chores before making their way to the River's End Saloon. From the outside, it looked rundown and dull, and the inside wasn't any improvement. The gloomy atmosphere was only enhanced by the stench of stale alcohol as they entered the establishment through the swinging double doors. Squared, wooden beams supported the upper floor. The walls were covered in a thick layer of dust, obscuring the sparse amount of paintings on the walls. Judging by the derelict condition of the place, it was clear it hadn't been maintained.

The barkeep was pouring a drink for a customer sitting at the long wooden bar. Both men barely glanced up and grunted, making it clear neither cared that there were new arrivals at the saloon. Across the way, there was a group of three men playing poker, who didn't even bother to look their way. Nolan's fellow co-workers had discussed that the saloon was infamous for brawls, but as they sidled up to the bar, it felt nearly abandoned.

"Where is everyone?" Nolan questioned with confusion as he glanced around the saloon. "You made this place sound like it was always packed with action. At the moment, I could hear a pin drop in this place."

"Another saloon opened on the other side of town last week," David explained. "They're probably all down there."

It didn't matter to Nolan. It made his ability to question John and Timothy much easier if he didn't have to fight for their attention. Hopefully, after a couple of well-supplied drinks, Nolan would get one of them to divulge a clue as to who was the thief.

"Since I'm the new guy, first round is on me.

Barkeep, we'd each like a glass of whiskey," Nolan requested.

"Thank you," each of the men cheered as the barkeep slid a glass to each of them. The depot workers took sips of their drinks and talked about the day and their families. After the second round of drinks, the men became louder, joking more harshly and discussing aspects about their wives that made Nolan uncomfortable. If it wasn't part of his real job to try to get to the bottom of the theft, he would have left the saloon to avoid hearing the foul talk.

By the fourth round of drinks, this time provided by Timothy, Nolan's co-workers were becoming foolish. It was only compounded by the fact that a fresh group of men from one of the nearby ranches stumbled into the saloon, and took seats at the other end of the bar.

"Barkeep, I'd like a round of bourbon for my friends," one of the cowboys slurred out. "We had to leave the other saloon because we got too handsy with the help."

One of the other cowboys cackled, then glanced around as if searching for something. "Where are the girls around here? Don't tell me none of them are working tonight."

"They caught a cold and can't work tonight," the barkeep informed them.

"Both of them?" one of the other cowboys asked with irritation. "No wonder no one's coming here anymore. Can't even keep girls in the saloon to serve the drinks."

"They'll be back to work in a couple of days," the barkeep explained, trying to appease the new customers. "In the meantime, I can give you a round of drinks on the house."

Nolan wished the cowboys would just go away. They seemed bound and determined to be contrary, and there was no way Nolan was going to be able to question his co-workers with them in the saloon. He wished they would just leave, but his gut told him it was only going to get worse now that they were there.

"Drinks alone aren't enough," the third cowboy bellowed in anger, slamming his fist down on the bar. "I want a pretty face to look at while I drink, and yours, barkeep, doesn't even begin to qualify as such."

"Can you just hush now," Timothy demanded with a heavy sigh. "Some of us just want to enjoy our drinks in peace."

"Mind your own business, old man," the third

cowboy snarled at Timothy. "This doesn't concern you."

"Don't talk to him like that," John yelled back, jumping up from his seat and nearly knocking Nolan over in the process, "or you're going to regret it."

"Boy, you best shut your mouth and sit back down," the other man barked out as he jumped up, moving towards John.

When John didn't do as the cowboy demanded, the cowboy lifted his fists in the air. Before Nolan knew what was happening, the cowboy was swinging at John.

Complete pandemonium ensued, both sets of men rushed to their feet and started fighting. Nolan didn't want to get involved, but he also knew if he didn't, it would set him back with his co-workers. If he had any chance of gaining their trust, he needed to fight alongside them. Nolan pulled back his arm and let his fist fly into the first face of the nearest cowboy, who happened to be fighting with John. The man grunted but didn't go down. Instead, he exchanged Nolan's blow for one of his own, his fist making contact with Nolan's jaw, causing Nolan to stagger backward from the sheer force of it. Brawls were not a part of his usual past time, and Nolan's face throbbed from the pulsating pain, but he ignored it. He steadied himself and pushed forward into the thick of the fight.

The men spilled out through the doors and onto the street. Fists were flying all around Nolan. He was about to swing again when the entire brawl was interrupted by gunfire. Everyone froze for a moment before turning to look at the sheriff with his two deputies by his side.

"That's enough of this," the sheriff shouted in an authoritative voice as he lowered his gun to his side. "The next man that takes a swing is going to jail. I won't have fighting in my town."

The men must have known the sheriff was serious because everyone complied. The cowboys trickled back into the saloon while the depot workers remained outside.

"Thanks for helping me. If you're ever in a similar situation, I'll do the same for you." John patted Nolan on the back. "You just proved you're one of us. You have to promise not to tell my wife, though," John begged Nolan, slurring the words as he spoke. "I promised her I would stop my antics now that the baby is coming, but trouble always manages to find me."

"I'm sure it's not that bad," Nolan comforted

with a sympathetic smile but made note that John, by his own admission, was always getting into trouble. This was it; now was Nolan's chance to ask John some questions that could lead to answers about the depot theft. Before a question could pass his lips though, Dina Stone and Georgia Boggs came rushing towards the men.

"What on earth is going on here?" Georgia shrieked out. "We heard the gunfire from the house, and couldn't believe our eyes when we looked out the window and saw you all in the street."

"You should all be ashamed of yourself," Dina rebuked. "Proper gentleman don't act like this. I expect all of you to get home to your wives. As for you, Timothy, you're coming with me right now." Dina marched over and wrapped her arm through her husband's, pulling him away from the group.

The rest of the depot workers were already shuffling off in different directions, and Nolan realized his plans to get answers were going to have to wait. He was going to have his own explaining to do when he got home and had to face Elsie.

Quietly, he entered the house, after debating what to tell his wife when he did. She was sitting on the couch reading a book. She looked up with a smile on her face, but it vanished quickly as her eyes fixed on his face. She jumped up from her seat and rushed over to him, gently letting her fingertips brush across the bruises that were already forming. "Good gravy, what happened to you?"

"It's nothing," Nolan quickly defended. "I went out with the men from the depot after work, hoping that a couple of drinks might loosen their lips."

"It seems it loosened more than their lips. Tell me you didn't get into a fight with them. Won't that make getting answers nearly impossible?"

"I didn't get in a fight with them. They got in a fight with a group of cowboys," Nolan explained. "I had to fight alongside them—it was the quickest way to get them to trust me."

"Well, I can't say I love the idea of my husband getting into brawls at the local saloon, but I suppose under the circumstances, I guess I understand why you did it." She took his hand and pulled him toward the kitchen table. "Come on, let me take care of your cuts."

Nolan took a seat at the table while Elsie headed over to the sink. She took a towel and wet it, then brought it back over to Nolan, bending down in front of him. Gingerly, she took the edge and brushed it along his jaw. Nolan tried not to flinch, but he couldn't help himself.

"Am I being too rough?" she questioned as she looked into his eyes with concern, her hand pausing and hovering over the next cut on the other side of his face.

"It's not your fault, it just stings something awful."

"I'm sorry about that. I'll try to be more gentle with the next cut." She finished cleaning the wounds, then moved on to applying ointment. As her hand moved along his face, he couldn't help but enjoy the feel of her soft touch against his skin, despite the occasional tinges of pain.

Nolan's hand moved up and closed over hers. "I like you taking care of me."

Elsie's eyes locked with his and the desire he was feeling was reflected in them. He moved towards her, the thought of kissing her perfect pink lips enticing him to close the small distance between them. Just as his mouth was about to claim hers, she put up her hands and placed them on his chest, stopping him. "I need to check on the stew." Elsie stood up and spun around, making a retreat towards the kitchen. "Why don't you go get changed before supper?"

Nolan did as his wife suggested, wondering the whole time what he did wrong to cause her to react in such a way. Had he been mistaken about what he thought he saw in her eyes? Was he alone in his attraction to her? If that were the case, he needed to be more careful in the future. It wouldn't be the first time he let his attraction for a beautiful woman lead him down a dangerous path; he couldn't afford to do it again.

CHAPTER FIVE

Ever since Nolan came close to kissing her, Elsie had been avoiding spending time alone with her husband. It wasn't that she didn't want him to kiss her; it was just the opposite. She was afraid if she let him, she would get too attached, and that was the last thing she needed. There was a strong possibility at the end of their case in Mitchell, he might very well want to call their marriage quits. If she let her heart get involved, losing him might be more than she could bear. It was better to keep her distance. The problem was, that was mighty hard when they were heading to the town social. Their purpose was to keep up their façade while they discreetly questioned the two remaining couples, but that didn't mean there wouldn't be dancing. How would she feel when Nolan held her in his arms? Would she be able to keep her heart from falling for him?

"Are you ready to go?" Nolan asked from across the hall.

Elsie couldn't help but notice how handsome her husband looked in his three-piece gray suit. It was the same one he wore on the first day he met her, and it looked even better than she remembered. She glanced down at her own dress, feeling for the first time, her own attire wasn't nearly as nice. What she wouldn't give to have a new dress. She hadn't had one since her mother passed away. She didn't have any money of her own, and she wasn't about to ask Nolan for any.

"I have something for you," Nolan said as he dipped into his room and came out with a box in his hands.

"What is it?" she questioned with surprise.

"Open it and find out."

She moved into her room and placed the box on the edge of her bed. She lifted the lid and pushed back the paper to reveal a gorgeous, plum gown. Her fingers ran along the soft, velvet fabric and black lace detailing, enjoying the texture of the contrasting materials. "Why did you do this?"

"I noticed you've been wearing the same couple of outfits, and figured it would be nice for you to have a new dress for social occasions and church."

"It's breathtaking," she gushed with joy as she pulled the gown free from the box and held it up against her frame. "It was so thoughtful of you."

"I figured since you're helping me with the case, it's the least I can do to say 'thank you.'"

Tears filled the corners of her eyes as she swished the bottom of the dress back and forth, imagining herself dancing in the dress later that evening.

"What's wrong? Did you change your mind? You don't like it?" Nolan asked with apprehension as his brows came together in a furrow.

She shook her head. "It's not that; I love it."

"Then what's the matter?" he probed further. "I want you to be happy—tell me what I can do to make you so."

"You're doing it. I haven't had a new dress since my mama passed away. My papa said that it was a waste of money, and told me to patch my old dresses. They were nearly falling apart when I came out here, but I thought getting a new dress was out of the question."

"Why? You're my wife now. It's my job to take

care of you, and part of that is making sure you have proper clothes. How about this next week, we go into town and I get you a couple of other items you need. I noticed your boots are wearing thin on the soles."

"I'd appreciate that," Elsie said with gratitude. Glancing down at the gown in her hands, she added, "Why don't you let me slip into your gift, and then I'll be right out."

Nolan left the room and closed the door behind him. A few moments later, Elsie was in her new dress, but no matter how hard she tried, she couldn't reach several of the back buttons. She bit her lip, debating what she should do. Deciding she didn't have another choice, she called out for her husband. "Do you think you can come in here and help with my buttons?"

From over her shoulder, she watched as Nolan hesitantly came back into the room. He moved towards her, reaching out and gently touching her back. As his hand brushed along her skin—merely separated by a thin shift—she could feel goose bumps prickle along her flesh, teasing her to wonder what it would be like to have his hands caress her without anything between them.

"These last couple of buttons are being difficult," he grumbled as he moved closer, his strong, thick physique pressing up against her smaller, delicate frame. His nearness caused a shiver to shimmy up her spine, and she could feel herself shake slightly. "I'm finished," he whispered as he pulled her around to face him. "Wow, that dress looks amazing. It's even better than I imagined when I picked it out."

"You imagined me in it?" she questioned with an arched eyebrow and smirk. "I'm not sure what to think of you envisioning me in a state of undress."

"I never said I imagined you changing into it," he corrected, "though now that you mention it, my mind can't help but think about such a tantalizing idea." He stretched out his hand and placed it on the side of her cheek. "I shouldn't admit this, but you've been taking up quite a bit of my thoughts lately."

"It goes both ways," she admitted, biting her bottom lip in apprehension as she realized what she just revealed to Nolan. As she looked into his eyes, she could see the desire reflected in them. Was this it? Was this the moment he was going to kiss her? She took in a deep breath and held it, anxiously waiting to see what he was going to do next.

"We should probably get going," Nolan stated,

dropping his hand to his side and stepping away from her.

She could feel the disappointment in the pit of her stomach, making her mad at herself. Why had she wanted him to kiss her so badly? This arrangement was most likely only temporary, and she didn't need to get her heart involved. The last thing she needed to do was to get hurt by letting herself fall for her husband.

"Let me get my shawl and purse, and then we can be on our way." Elsie turned away so he couldn't see the effect he had on her. She busied herself gathering up the items before heading into the kitchen to grab her pie for the auction, which was cooling on the counter.

"When are you going to make me one of those?" he asked, looking over her shoulder at the perfectly flaky treat.

"Maybe you'll just need to bid on this one," she teased with a wink. "That way, at least I know someone is going to, and I won't be embarrassed when no one else does."

"That won't happen. I've been bragging to everyone at work how great your pie is. I'm sure everyone in town knows by now," Nolan vowed. "No, if I'm ever going to get the chance to try your pie, you're going to have to make me my own."

"I suppose if it means that much to you, I can make you one this weekend."

"I could help," Nolan offered, reaching out his arm to her. She placed her free hand in the crook. "I'm not the best baker, but I can offer you an extra set of hands."

"I just might take you up on that. I could always use a good assistant. Plus, if it means I get to spend some time with you, it would be worth it." Her eyes rounded with embarrassment as her eyes locked with his. Even though she enjoyed her husband's company, she wasn't sure where she stood with him. She turned her head to the side, afraid of the rejection she might see written across his face.

They made their way over to the town square next to the church. The place was already bustling with the women preparing the area for the social.

"There you are. You should have been here an hour ago," Dina barked out.

Elsie bit back her defense that she was arriving right at the time she had been told. She wanted to accuse the other woman of purposely giving her the wrong time, but Elsie knew it would only cause more problems than do her any good. It was better to let the scolding wash over her and move on. She wanted to keep Dina on her good side—if that were at all possible—so she could question her later.

"Why don't you come set your pie down," Cara suggested as she came up to the two women. "It looks magnificent by the way. I can see it fetching a pretty penny in the auction." Dina made a "humph" noise under her breath as she spun around in a huff. "I hate to say this, but Dina is in a particularly snarly mood this afternoon." Her eyes drifted down to Elsie's gown and a smile of approval spread across her lips. "That dress is gorgeous. Is it new?"

Elsie nodded. "My husband surprised me with it for the social."

"Well, he did a wonderful job," Cara stated with appreciation. "He has great taste."

Nolan's cheeks turned red, most likely because the women were talking about him like he wasn't there. "I see a few of the men helping with the wooden stage for the band; I think I will go help them." Nolan gently pulled free from Elsie's hand and took off across the town square.

Cara escorted her over to the pie table that was decorated with a blue and white gingham tablecloth as well as three vases of flowers. She took Elsie's pie and put it in the center of the table. "Here, it deserves to be the star. I can't wait to see you beat Dina in the auction."

Elsie was about to object, but two of the other women arrived to place their pies on the table. The next hour was spent rushing around making sure everything was ready for the big event. By the time the women were done, the townsfolk were arriving for the start of the festivities.

Dina took a spot center stage, her head held high with pride. "Good afternoon, fellow Mitchellers, it's good to see so many here to support the women auxiliary's efforts to raise money for the much-needed schoolhouse. We know many of you have a sweet tooth, and we have just the fix for it. This afternoon, we have every sugar-lover's dream. Our town's very best pie-makers have each brought their finest creations, and you have the chance to take them home with you tonight. All you have to do is have the highest bid at the auction." Dina gestured for a gray-haired man to come up beside her. "Mayor Reynolds will be conducting the auction, so get ready, ladies and gentlemen, for the First Annual Mitchell Pie Auction."

The mayor had the first pie brought up from

the stage. He read the information from the paper that came with it, and the townsfolk started to bid.

Immediately, Elsie was worried. She hadn't prepared anything to be read about her pie. Did Dina purposely forget to tell her to do that, too? She glanced across the crowd and her eyes locked with Dina. She immediately knew her suspicions were correct. She'd been sabotaged before the auction even started.

A couple of more pies were purchased before Dina's came up for auction. She was looking around the crowd, giving dirty looks to townsfolk in a way that made it clear that they needed to bid on her pie or there would be consequences.

Elsie needed to do something before her pie came up for auction. Perhaps there was a pen and paper by the pie table she could use. "Excuse me, Nolan, I have to go take care of something really quickly." Elsie took off towards the pie table, her eyes darting around for anything she might be able to use to write down a description.

"Looking for something?" Dina asked with a cackle. "I can assure you, you're not going to find anything—or anyone for that matter—around here to help you."

"Why are you being so mean to me?" Elsie

blurted out, tired of the other woman constantly coming after her in such a mean-spirited way. "What did I ever do to you?"

"Whatever do you mean? I'm simply telling you that I highly doubt your pie is going to fetch a huge sum when no one knows that it's supposedly an award-winning one. You might as well accept that my pie is going to receive the highest bid."

Elsie could feel tears sting the corners of her eyes, but she rapidly blinked them away. There was no way she was going to let this woman make her cry.

"Apparently, this auction means far more to you than it does to me. I simply wanted to help raise money for the schoolhouse. You, on the other hand, seem to think there's more to it than that." Elsie brushed past the other woman, deciding she didn't care if she got to question her after all. In her mind, Dina's despicable behavior proved that she was most certainly married to the thief at the depot.

"Are you all right?" Nolan asked as she came back to take her spot next to him.

"No, but it doesn't matter," she whispered. "I just want this auction to be over, so we can go home."

"I thought you were looking forward to the

dancing?" Nolan probed with confusion. "I have to admit, so was I."

"It's not that. Dina is going out of her way to ruin my pie's chances in the auction. She purposely didn't tell me that I needed to provide a description for my pie."

"Well, we can't have that," Nolan said, pulling out a pen and notepad from his pocket. "I suppose it helps I have to write down a lot of notes, doesn't it?" He handed them over to her, giving her just enough time to write a description and hand it to the mayor as her pie was brought forward.

"My, my, we have a special treat right here. This delicious cherry pie was created by a two-time blue-ribbon winner, Elsie Winslow. Her pies were known to be the best throughout her county in Mississippi, and she's proud to be sharing her award-winning dessert with us out here in the Dakotas."

Immediately, rapid bids began pouring in. The prices out-did almost all of the previous pies besides Dina's. Just as she thought her pie was about to go to one of the ranchers, she heard her own husband place an even higher bid on it.

"What are you doing?" Elsie gasped between clenched teeth. "I already told you I'd make you your own pie this weekend."

"I decided I want this one," he stated firmly. "I want to make sure your pie goes for the highest amount, and that stuffy fussbudget doesn't get her rotten pie to win when it doesn't deserve it."

The bidding went on a couple of more times, but when the rancher offered a full dollar more than what Dina's pie went for, Elsie squeezed Nolan's arm. "You can stop now."

"Are you sure?" he asked, looking down at her. "Because I'm willing to pay whatever it takes to make you happy."

She shook her head. "Really, I'm good."

Nolan let out a sigh and dropped his hand. "I suppose a dollar is enough to make Mrs. Stone seethe with anger for a few weeks."

The rancher ended up with the pie, and everyone else let out defeated "ahs" as the award-winning dessert left the stage. The rest of the pies were auctioned off. As the last pie left the stage, Georgia announced that nearly half the money needed to build the schoolhouse had been raised through the event. The crowd cheered and clapped with excitement as the band took to the stage.

"Congrats," Nolan said with a smile. "I can't believe I'm married to the best pie-maker in all of Mitchell."

"I wouldn't go that far." Dina came up to them with her hands on her hips, her husband by her side with a sympathetic grimace on his face. "I saw what you did, Mr. Winslow, bidding your wife's pie up like that. She wouldn't have gotten the highest amount if it hadn't been for you."

"Oh no, Dina, don't be like that," her husband coddled. "There's no reason to act like this. How about I take you to the dress shop tomorrow and let you pick out anything you want? I'll use the new money I came into; just promise me you'll let this go."

The new information immediately made Elsie perk up. New money? Where did he get it? How much did he have? Could Nolan use that information to prove Mr. Stone was behind the theft at the depot?

"Anything I want?" Dina asked with an arched eyebrow, her haughty stance simmering down into a cool demeanor.

"Yes, anything for you, sweetheart," her husband promised.

"Fine, I suppose this silly old pie auction doesn't mean anything in the grand scheme of things." Dina stretched out her hand to her husband. "It's time for dancing anyhow."

The Stones sauntered off towards the area where couples were gathering for the next part of the night.

Elsie turned to talk with her husband about the information they just overheard, but before she could, the other women from the auxiliary came rushing up to her.

"I can't believe how well your pie did," Julia gushed with awe. "My own pie only got about a fraction of what yours made, which isn't surprising since I burnt the edges."

"I could teach you how to avoid that," Elsie offered.

"Really? That would be wonderful."

"I'd like to have the same lesson," Barbara requested. "I'm horrible at making pies, too."

"How about I have both of you over on Tuesday for a lesson?"

Both women nodded with wide smiles. "And I'll have you over to my home for lunch to say 'thank you' on Friday," Barbara returned.

"That sounds lovely. I can't wait."

"If you'll excuse us ladies, I think it's about time I dance with my wife." Nolan pulled Elsie towards the area where everyone was swaying to the music.

They danced to several fast songs before a

slower one started to play. As it did, Nolan gathered her into his arms, pulling her snugly against his muscular frame. "You smell like wildflowers and honey," he mumbled against her cheek. "Ever since the first time I met you, I couldn't shake your scent from my mind. I keep trying to put distance between us, but no matter what I do, I keep finding myself coming back to you over and over again."

"Is that so bad," she whispered in return. "Maybe that's how it's supposed to be."

"I'm not sure I can fight whatever is going on between us anymore." His mouth moved towards hers, stopping only inches away as he looked deep into her eyes.

"Then don't," she stated bluntly, hoping he would close the minuscule distance between them and sear her lips with his own.

Before it could happen though, there was an outburst of rain, made even more violent with gusts of wind that whipped the cold, wet liquid against them. Nolan removed his jacket and put it over both their heads as they made their escape, running towards their house.

Once inside, he shook the rain from his jacket and placed it on the coat rack beside the door. "I don't know if I will ever get used to the way weather changes so quickly here in the Dakotas."

"I agree, that storm came out of nowhere," Elsie acknowledged as she looked at her husband. Part of her hoped he would continue were they left off at the dance, but instead, he turned and headed towards the hall that led to the bedrooms.

"It's been a long day. I think we should both get some rest."

She hid her disappointment and did as her husband suggested, moving down the hall to her own room. As she lay in her large, empty bed across the hall from him, however, she wondered what it would be like if it didn't stay that way forever. What would it be like if one day she shared her bed with her husband? Of course, that would mean Nolan would have to let their relationship progress from a partnership into one of romance, and it seemed every time they got close to that happening, he put a stop to it. What would it take for him to finally give in to what they both wanted?

Elsie placed her hand out to the side, letting her fingers run along the cool, cotton fabric, as she hoped and prayed that she wouldn't be alone in it for the rest of her life.

After talking with Elsie the next morning, Nolan decided that he would make an opportunity to discuss the other man's new money with Timothy when he went back to work on Monday.

As they spent time together at church, and later at lunch at the café, Nolan couldn't help but admire his wife. There was more than meets the eye when it came to her. Elsie was tough and resilient, never giving up once she set her mind to something, and smart as a whip, too, with just the right amount of humor thrown in. She was determined to help him get to the bottom of the theft, and her observations had proven useful more than once. He'd nearly kissed her when they were dancing. It was scary because he knew it would mean more than it ever had with the dalliances he had back in New York.

The weekend sped by fast, and by Monday morning, Nolan was contemplating how Elsie was the perfect match for him in every way, and he could find himself letting their relationship become real if he wasn't careful. That wouldn't be fair to either of them though. Between his uncertainty with the agency and his past hanging over his head, Nolan couldn't let himself complicate things further by falling in love with Elsie. It's why he was grateful when the rain—quite literally—slapped him in the face, reminding him that developing romantic feelings for Elsie was out of the question.

"Are you listening to me, Nolan?" John asked with an irritated tone. "I asked you twice if you're coming out with us after work today."

Nolan nodded, forcing himself to stop thinking about Elsie and to focus on doing his job; his real job, that was. Going out with the men would be the perfect chance to question Timothy about the money. "I wouldn't miss it."

John chuckled as he smacked Nolan on the shoulder. "Good, because I like knowing you're there to back me up."

"Are you planning to get in another fight?" Nolan inquired sarcastically.

"Planning, no, will it happen, possibly, which is why it's great you're coming along with us."

"All right, boys, it's time to get back to work," Timothy chastised as he came up to them. "We need to get the rest of these items put away in the warehouse until the train going west shows up tomorrow."

The men did as their boss ordered and made quick work of putting away the last of the cargo. By the end of it, everyone was exhausted, but it didn't keep them from heading over to the saloon after they were done.

They entered the River's End to find everything as they had the week before. The barkeep was pouring a drink for a single customer sitting at the bar, and the same gamblers were playing cards in the back.

"I don't see how this place stays open," Nolan mumbled under his breath.

"They might be losing some business to the new saloon, but they still have the best whiskey in town," Timothy stated firmly as the depot workers sidled up to the bar. "I'm proud of the work you did today. First-round is on me, boys."

The men ordered their drinks and talked about the work at the depot. By the third round of drinks, the men seemed to be looser with their words, cracking jokes and poking fun at one another.

Nolan saw his opportunity to question Timothy and took it. "The other day, you mentioned coming into some new money, Timothy. Do you have a side-job lined up? I could really use the extra income to buy Elsie the household items and clothes she wants."

"I wish I could help you out, Nolan, but how I

got my new money wasn't from any job," Timothy confessed.

This was it, Timothy was going to tell him what he'd been digging around for. The money had to come from the proceeds after selling the stolen items. Nolan had to play his cards right though if he wanted Timothy to admit the truth. If Nolan appeared too eager, he might avoid confessing. He leaned ever-so-slightly forward and asked nonchalantly, "How did you come by it then?"

"My great uncle passed away and left me some money in his will. Dina and I have been deciding what to do with it over the last couple of months, and finally decided on expanding our house."

Nolan tried to hide his disappointment at the news. It wasn't what he expected to hear. He would of course have Agent Stansbury confirm the inheritance. If it was true, it most likely meant Timothy wasn't behind the theft, which left him with only one final suspect. Nolan looked down the bar at the blond man sitting at the end of it. Was the youngest member of their team the one behind the theft? Of all his co-workers, Nolan had grown the closest to John. The thought of having to put his friend behind bars at the end of his investigation didn't sit well with Nolan. He knew, however, he had to do his duty, whether he wanted to or not. If John was guilty, he would find the evidence and do what was needed.

For the rest of the evening, he looked for a chance to speak with John privately, but the chance never manifested. By the time they were leaving the saloon, Nolan felt defeated until he remembered that Elsie was having lunch with John's wife later that week. When he arrived home, he couldn't wait to explain the situation to Elsie.

"And you're certain it's not Timothy?" Elsie inquired a second time as she took a sip of her tea.

"Well, I'll have Agent Stansbury confirm it to be certain, but if Timothy's story is true, he's been deciding what to do with his inheritance for months. Why would he need to steal from the depot if he has plenty of money already? I think it primarily eliminates him as our thief, making John a more likely suspect."

"That makes sense. I suppose that means you want me to see what I can find out from Barbara when I go over to her house."

"Yes, that's exactly what I was thinking since you've offered to help in whatever way you can."

Elsie set her cup down and tilted her head to the

side, her green eyes twinkling with excitement. "So, what you're saying is that you need me."

"I thought you already knew that," he whispered in a far-more raspy voice then he planned to use. He swallowed a couple of times, trying to release the lump lodged in his throat, as his eyes drifted down to stare at his wife's perfect, pink lips. The temptation to kiss her was nearly more than he could resist, and he found himself jumping to his feet to avoid doing just that. "I'm going to go clean up for supper."

Nolan took the next half hour to calm his nerves, and prepare himself to return to Elsie's side at the kitchen table. Every time he thought he got his racing feelings for his wife under control, she managed to get under his skin again. He wondered how long he was going to be able to hold out before his desire to be with her took away all forms of reason.

CHAPTER SIX

As Elsie nibbled on a piece of cherry pie, she watched the young pregnant woman sitting across from her do the same. Elsie wondered what would happen to Barbara and her baby if her husband was behind the theft? Did she have a family to go back to somewhere? If she did, would they want her once they found out what her husband did? In her gut, Elsie knew that if John was the criminal they were looking for, it wasn't going to end well for his wife and child. Elsie had come to consider Barbara a friend, and the idea of ruining the other woman's life made her sick to her stomach.

"What do you think of the pie?" Barbara inquired, interrupting Elsie's thoughts. "I tried to do exactly what you said from the lesson you gave me on Monday. Did I do a good job?" Her friend anxiously bit her bottom lip and her brows bunched together as she waited for Elsie's verdict.

"You did a great job," Elsie praised, holding back the fact that the other woman baked the pie a little too long, and the crust was drier than it should be because of it.

"Really, or are you just being a nice friend? The crust isn't nearly as flaky or buttery as I remember yours being." Barbara shook her head, a look of frustration clearly written across her face. "I'm just glad that John didn't marry me expecting a good cook or baker. He'd be sadly mistaken if he had."

"We all have different gifts," Elsie consoled her friend. She glanced around the room at the pretty figurines and paintings that looked new and rather expensive. She seized the opportunity to ask the other woman about them. "Like your fine decorating sense; you really know how to make a house a home."

"You think so?" Barbara asked as she raised her eyebrows and let her own eyes wander around the room. "I wasn't sure about some of my recent purchases, but John insisted that with his pay raise from work, I should use a bit of the money to freshen the place up. He also insisted on a couple of new dresses for me, since I've been gaining weight due to the baby."

A pay raise? That didn't sound right to Elsie. From what Nolan told her about the men at the depot, John was the newest worker. At barely a year there, she highly doubted it warranted a raise. Accusing Barbara's husband of lying would only raise suspicion, however, and might very well tip him off if her friend was to bring it up to him at a later time. No, Elsie needed to wait. She needed to tell Nolan first so he could look into the story to confirm one way or another the accounting for the new items. In the meantime, she would continue to pretend everything was exactly as it was before. "Well, you did an excellent job of picking all of it out. I wish I had nearly as keen an eye as you do, Barbara."

"Thank you, Elsie, that's mighty kind of you to say so, but sometimes I wonder if I'm doing all of this right. I just want to be a good wife and mother." Barbara patted her pregnant stomach as a look of worry spread across her face.

A pang of guilt filled Elsie's heart. Barbara was being vulnerable with her, and she was spending time with the other woman under false pretenses.

Elsie wished she could be honest with Barbara about her own insecurities, but that would mean divulging the truth about her past and how she ended up married to Nolan. That couldn't happen if they were going to be able to successfully solve the case. Despite how hard it might be, she needed to continue to pretend so she could prove her worth to Nolan and convince him they were better together than apart.

"Don't be so hard on yourself. You're already a tremendous wife, and I'm sure you'll be just as wonderful a mother."

"What about you? Any plans to start your own family any time soon?" Barbara probed with a smile. "I think you'd make a terrific mother."

Elsie shifted in her seat, her eyes dropping to the table. "That's kind of you to say, but I'm not sure how Nolan feels about children."

"You haven't discussed it?" she asked in a way that made it clear she was shocked by the fact.

With a shake of her head, Elsie explained, "I was a mail-order bride when I came out here. We didn't really get into any of that before we were married."

"How about since then? Starting a family is the next step in your marriage, after all," Barbara pointed out, ignorant of the fact that Elsie and Nolan's relationship didn't follow a normal pattern, no matter how much she wanted him to love her the way a true husband loved his wife.

Elsie didn't know what to say, and rather than say something that would give away why they hadn't discussed something so key in a marriage, she jumped up from her seat, ready to flee the uncomfortable situation. "I need to head home and start supper."

Barbara stood quickly and reached out towards Elsie. "I can see I upset you. I'm sorry for pushing you about the matter. Please, don't be mad at me."

Elsie took in several deep breaths, forcing herself to calm down before responding. "It's not your fault; I just worry Nolan and I want very different things. If that's the case, I don't know what it means for our marriage."

On her way back home, she couldn't help but think about what Barbara brought to light. Elsie was afraid that she and Nolan would never be on the same page when it came to their future. She wanted to be a wife, in every sense of the word to him, but every time she thought he might want it too, he pushed her away.

Once home, she started a pot of stew, then set

about her other chores while she waited for Nolan to get home from work. When he did, she told him about her lunch with Barbara.

"You did good, Elsie."

"Is that an admission that I finally did something right for this case?" she asked with mirth written across her face. "If I didn't hear it with my own ears, I'd hardly believe it."

"Don't let it go to your head now," he teased back, "but yes, you're proving to be quite the asset on this case. I'm not sure if I would be able to find out the truth without you. On Monday, I can check the records in the depot office and see if John actually got a pay raise. If he didn't, then I can confront him with the truth, and hopefully, get a confession. This case should be wrapped up in a couple of days if everything goes well."

Elsie knew she should be excited by the fact that they were solving their first case quickly, but she couldn't help but acknowledge that also meant that there was a chance Nolan would want to end their arrangement. Even though she had helped him, was it enough to convince him that she was a worthy partner?

"Is there anything else I can do?"

Nolan shook his head. "You've done plenty.

How about I take you out to eat tomorrow to celebrate the good job you've done?"

"Will we be going to the café?"

He gave her a mischievous grin, sidestepping a direct answer. "You let me worry about that."

The brick building of the Hotel Magnifique came into view as Nolan guided Elsie towards the far end of Main Street. He glanced over at his wife, who was looking at the building with curiosity. Excitement pulsated through him as he anticipated Elsie's reaction to his surprise. He stopped walking and turned to face the hotel on the corner of the street.

"Why are we at a hotel?" Elsie questioned with confusion. "I thought you were taking me somewhere to eat."

"I am," he said, pulling her into the hotel. He guided her through the lobby and towards the back, were a fancily scrolled sign read, *Buvette*, with "the finest dining experience in the West" neatly written below the name.

"We're eating here?" Elsie inquired with raised eyebrows as she stiffened against his frame. "I had no idea that such a place existed in Mitchell."

"I asked around town if there were any gourmet restaurants nearby, and Timothy mentioned this place. He said he took Dina here for their last wedding anniversary."

"Well, despite the fact that my nemesis enjoys this place, I think I will still give it a try. After all, it's been my dream since before my mama passed away to partake in a meal made by a gourmet chef."

"You're in for a real treat then. Chef Laurent came from France and worked for years in New Orleans before coming out West to start a French restaurant in the frontier. Everyone thought he was crazy when he started this place in the Dakotas, but now it's one of the best-known places around—at least according to what Timothy told me."

"I just hope I don't make a fool of myself in there," she whispered as he escorted her through the front door. "Are we dressed nice enough?" Her eyes darted down to look at her attire.

Nolan let out a chuckle before nodding his head. "Certainly; why do you think I requested you to wear your plum gown?"

"And that's why you're wearing your Sunday suit," she pointed out with a knowing smile. "You had all of this planned."

A waiter was standing just inside the door and

greeted them with a friendly grin as they entered through the glass doors. "Welcome to Buvette. Will it be just the two of you this evening?"

Nolan nodded. "Yes, we're here to celebrate our nuptials. We never got a proper wedding celebration, so tonight I'm treating my new wife to whatever she wants."

Elsie looked up at him from her place by his side. An appreciative smile formed on her pretty lips, and if they had been alone, he would have leaned down and kissed her right on the spot. Instead, he returned the smile and squeezed the top of her hand where it rested in the crook of his arm.

"Well, then, we're glad you decided to choose Buvette as your destination to celebrate. Please, follow me." The waiter gestured for them towards the back of the restaurant.

He seated them at a table by a window and handed them each a menu. "What would you like to drink?"

"Would you care to share a bottle of wine?" Nolan offered as he looked over the edge of his menu at Elsie.

"I'm not sure how it tastes, since I've never had any, but if you think I will like it, I'll give it a try."

"I think you will," Nolan assured her. "Besides,

it pairs well with food." Then turning to the waiter, he added, "We'll take a bottle of your best red wine, please."

"I'll be right back with that, sir, and then I will take your order."

The waiter turned around and scurried off, leaving them alone. "This menu goes on and on. I have no idea what to order. What do you think I would like?" Elsie inquired as she scanned the menu.

"Why would you think to ask me?"

"You mentioned once, you spent time in fancy restaurants in New York." Elsie peeked over her menu at him with a perplexed look on her face. "You haven't told me much about your past or why you came out West. What little you did, left me with more questions than it did answers."

Nolan's brows lowered as he contemplated his response, his breath hitching in his chest as he thought about revealing what happened to him back in New York. He didn't want Elsie's opinion of him to change, and if he told her the truth, he was certain it would. "I'd prefer to forget about my past. I would rather focus on here, now, with you."

Before Elsie could say anything, the waiter returned with their wine. After pouring them both a glass, he took their order, before scurrying off a second time.

Nolan was relieved when Elsie didn't bring up his past again. Instead, they spent the rest of the meal discussing the case, as well as the town and the people in it. The conversation flowed effortlessly, proving to Nolan that every moment he spent with Elsie was a moment well spent.

Once the meal was over, Nolan helped Elsie by wrapping her shawl around her shoulders as they stood from the table.

"Thank you for bringing me here," she said with a smile. "I never thought I would have a chance to enjoy a place like this. It was kind of you to give me such a thoughtful surprise."

Nolan's heart warmed under Elsie's praise. He didn't realize how much he wanted to please her until she made it clear he had. "I'm glad you liked it."

"The night has been so nice. I was thinking, why does it have to end? How about we head over to the waterfront and walk along the river's edge?"

"I would love that," Elsie replied with a smile.

Just as they exited the hotel, Timothy and Dina Stone came into view. Dina had a scowl plastered across her face as she glared at them in a way that made it clear that she wasn't pleased to see them. "What are you doing at the hotel, Mrs. Winslow? You weren't eating at *Buvette*, were you?" Elsie stiffened against Nolan's side and squeezed his arm where her hand rested. When she didn't answer, Dina continued on her tirade. "It isn't bad enough you're trying to poach my friends, but now you're trying to take over my favorite restaurant?" Dina accused.

"What are you talking about?" Elsie gulped out, her eyes rounding with shock as she stared at the other woman.

"I know you had Georgia and Barbara over to show them how to make pies last week, and just the other day, you went to Barbara's house for lunch. Don't think you can come in to my town and try to take over. I won't have it," Dina snapped out, her eyes flashing with anger.

"I didn't mean to cause any problems, honest," Elsie defended, tears filling the corners of her eyes as her bottom lip trembled.

"I don't care what you meant to do—you're disrupting my happy life, and I won't stand for it. You need to stay away from my friends and the places I care about."

"You need to stop attacking my wife right this

instant," Nolan growled out. "What type of lady behaves the way you do? Look at yourself and you'll see that your friends are tired of how you treat them. You can't go around acting in such a manner and expect it to go without consequences."

"How dare you talk to me like that. Why I—"

"That's enough," Timothy interrupted his wife, giving her a stern look that Nolan had never seen on the other man's face when dealing with Dina. "We're going home to discuss how things are going to change going forward. I'm tired of being embarrassed by you."

Timothy took his wife by the arm and escorted her away from the hotel. Once they were good and gone, Nolan turned towards Elsie. "Never have I met a more loathsome woman. Are you all right?"

Elsie nodded. "I can't wait until this case is over and I can leave all this unpleasantness behind me."

Nolan's stomach clenched with dread at the thought of her leaving him behind, too. "You don't count me as part of that unpleasantness, do you?"

"Of course, not. I hope by now, you realize how much I enjoy your company."

"I'm glad to hear it," he said, reaching out and placing his hand on the side of her face. "I enjoy being with you, too, Elsie."

She stepped closer to him, her hands moving up to rest on his chest. "Thank you for standing up for me. I've never had anyone do that for me."

"You're welcome." Nolan couldn't help but find her irresistible, and before he knew what he was doing, his lips were moving towards hers until they caressed them in the gentlest of motions. She sighed against his mouth as her arms drifted up and curled around his neck, urging him to deepen the kiss. He wrapped his arms around her waist and pulled her close, savoring every sensation stirring inside him as he kissed Elsie for the first time.

When she pulled back, part of him wanted to stop her, but he knew this wouldn't be the last time he kissed his wife. Now that he knew how wonderful it felt to do it, he planned on kissing her as much as possible.

CHAPTER SEVEN

Elsie was humming to herself as she went about her preparation for supper. She wanted the meal to be perfect when Nolan arrived home. Tonight was the night she was going to tell him how she felt. He deserved to know how much she admired him, and how that esteem had turned into love as their relationship progressed.

Nolan was thoughtful, kind, and steadfast. He put her needs above his own, making every effort to make her happy. She hadn't been sure what being married was going to bring, especially when it started out as a marriage of convenience for his job, but she never knew she could be so contented as she was being Nolan's wife.

It wasn't just the big displays of affection either.

It was the little things he did that made her heart fill with joy. Just yesterday, he brought her a bouquet of wildflowers he picked just for her on his way home from the mercantile. She glanced over at the fragrant beauties sitting in the vase centered on the kitchen table. Her heart skipped a beat as she smiled to herself about how sweet the gesture was.

The noise of the front door opening interrupted Elsie's musings. She glanced at the clock hanging on the wall, and realized it was too early for Nolan to be returning. Did a breeze push the door open? Was it possible she didn't shut it properly when she came back from the mercantile earlier that morning?

She walked the short distance from the kitchen, but froze just as she entered the living room, fear seizing her heart. Elsie could hardly believe her eyes as she saw her father march towards her with an angry look on his face. "Papa, what are you doing here?"

"I came to take you back home where you belong. You're lucky I'm not going to kill you—though the thought did cross my mind—for nearly costing me my deal with Arthur Dorin."

"How did you find me?" she squeaked out with

fright, upset because she thought she covered her tracks well.

"When I found out that you ran off, I questioned everyone you were friends with. It took some convincing from Sarah's own papa's belt, but she finally admitted that you were planning to be a mail-order bride for a man out West. I knew the only way you could arrange it was to send a telegraph, so I questioned the postmaster."

Elsie crossed her arms and narrowed her eyes. "He doesn't like you though. Why would he tell you where I went?"

"You're right. He didn't want to at first, so I had a few of the men from the gambling hall who owed me a debt make it clear he didn't have a choice. A couple of broken ribs later, he spilled the information like a can of beans."

Her papa looked pleased with himself, but his pride over the violence he brandished only made her stomach churn with disgust. "That still doesn't explain how you tracked me down here."

"I went to that Pinkerton office, but again, I couldn't get anywhere. I waited until they left, and broke into the office. I went through the files and found out where your new 'husband' was assigned and came out here after you."

"Where did you get the money? We never had enough to even get me a dress or celebrate Christmas. How did you come by all the money to come out here to the Dakotas?"

"How do you think? I stole money from a few people in Laurel, then stole the rest from that Pinkerton agency. I couldn't live with all the pitying looks I was getting around town when my own daughter ran off on me. I knew I had to get you back and make you marry Dorin to make things right again."

Elsie's papa sounded crazy. How could he possibly think that he could make her do anything, let alone return with him to Laurel to marry another man? "I can't do that, Papa. I'm already married."

"We can have that annulled. No one will believe you married this Pinkerton fellow on your own accord," her papa said as he flicked his wrist in the air. "He's trained in trickery, and he must have bamboozled you into pretending to be his wife."

"But it isn't pretend, Papa. I'm his wife, and I want to keep being his wife. I love him," she blurted out and realized as she said the words out loud it was the truth. She loved Nolan, and when the time was right, she was going to tell him, too.

"Come now, girl, I'll have none of that nonsense." He closed the final distance between them and yanked her by the arm towards the door. "You're my daughter, and you're leaving with me."

"No, she isn't," she heard Nolan yell from the front door.

Elsie glanced past her papa and was relieved to see Nolan standing there with a pistol in his hand. He was aiming it at her papa, and had a look in his eye, that if pressed, he wouldn't hesitate to pull the trigger. "Let my wife go right now."

Elsie's papa spun around, pulling Elsie behind him, shocked to see Nolan standing behind him. "Stay out of this, boy. It has nothing to do with you."

"It has everything to do with me since Elsie is my wife. I'm not letting you make her leave when she clearly doesn't want to."

"She doesn't know what she wants. You've confused her with all your deception. It's what men like you do, trick young girls into doing your bidding. If you don't let me take my daughter, right this instant, I'll tell all the nice townsfolk around here that you're a Pinkerton agent, and why you really came here."

"Don't threaten him," Elsie shouted at her papa

as she continued to try to pull away from his grasp. "My husband is a good man, and I won't have you jeopardize his future because of me."

"My job as a Pinkerton agent doesn't matter as much as your safety, Elsie. I'd gladly give it up to keep you from harm."

"How sweet; you two sound like a couple of lovesick children, but let me be clear, I will ruin your lives if you don't do what I say," Elsie's papa threatened.

"If you try to tell anyone around here about Nolan's real identity, I'll tell the sheriff that you broke into the Pinkerton agency, stole information, and their petty cash. He might lose his job, but you'll spend years behind bars," Elsie promised with resolve in her heart.

"You wouldn't dare to do that to me," her papa bellowed, rage flaming in his eyes as he let out a list of curse words to finish his point.

"Elsie has made her stance on the matter clear." Nolan moved over and wrapped his arm around his wife's shoulders. "We want you to leave and never come back. There's no place for you in our lives."

"Is that so, Elsie? Do you never want to see your papa again?"

For the first time, there was a hint of hurt in his

voice, and she could clearly see the testament of many troubled years etched across his wrinkled face. It didn't change, however, what he tried to do to her back in Laurel, or the reason he came here to try to do it again. He didn't love her, only what he could get from using her.

"I think it's best," Elsie stammered out. Raising her chin she added, "I have a new life with my husband, and I'm happy with it. Nolan doesn't view me as a commodity that he can use for his own gain."

"I read the file at that Pinkerton office, and your husband only needs you for this job. Once he's finished with it, he'll be finished with you, mark my words. When he is, don't come cryin' to me. You've made your bed, now you're gonna have to sleep in it." Her papa spun around and marched out of the house in a huff, slamming the front door behind him. The pictures on the wall rattled, and one even went crashing to the ground, splintering the wood frame, and spraying out glass in all directions.

"Oh no," Elsie gasped out as she rushed over and bent down to pick up the shards. Tears were streaming down her cheeks, partly from what happened with her papa, and partly because his parting words struck a chord in Elsie's own skeptical heart. She worried that the life she was building with Nolan was only temporary, and all of it would come crashing down one day. Would he be done with her once he was done with the case?

She continued to pick up the pieces of glass with her right hand and placed them in the palm of her left one, but one landed wrong, cutting her tender flesh. "Ouch," she cried out, between sobs.

Nolan rushed to her side and flipped her hand over, causing the glass to fall back on the ground. "There's no need for that right now." He pulled out his handkerchief and wrapped it around her wound. "You're in no condition to be cleaning this up. I bet you can't even see straight through all those tears."

"Stop that," she gulped out, a small hiccup escaping her lips as she tried to brush away the tears with the back of her uninjured hand.

"Stop what?" he asked, his eyes meeting hers, and he continued to gently hold onto her wounded hand.

"Being so sweet. When you do that, you make me forget that this arrangement is simply a business necessity."

"Don't listen to him, Elsie. He doesn't know what he's talking about. It might have started out that way, but you mean far more to me than that now."

"I do?" she asked, unable to hide the hope that not only crept into her voice but also her heart. There was a fluttering in her stomach as she sucked in a breath and held it, waiting for him to confirm that he felt for her the same way she did him.

"I'm smitten with you, Elsie. I'm not sure how it happened, or when, but it's true." Nolan leaned over and kissed Elsie, but this wasn't like the kiss from the other night. It was filled with passion, and it pushed away all other thoughts than the need to be consumed by her husband.

Elsie reached out and wrapped her arms around him as he pulled her close. She could feel her heart thudding against her chest, her pulse racing as she enjoyed every minute of being in her husband's arms and the feel of his soft lips against her own.

Nolan pulled back only long enough to stand up and take her by the hand. He pulled her towards the hall, stopping right in the middle. "Do you want to continue this in one of our rooms?"

Elsie bit her lip, not realizing that their kiss would lead to a choice like this. Before she could answer him, she smelled the acidic smell of smoke fill her nostrils. Her eyes widened as she yanked her hand away and turned around, rushing towards the kitchen. The pot of food on the stove was billowing dark gray smoke, enough so that the entire kitchen was thick with it. "Good gravy, supper is burning," she gasped out in frustration. She grabbed the nearby rag and yanked the pot from the stove, trying her best to keep the smoke from burning her eyes. She dropped it into the sink, angry that the perfect meal she'd been planning was now ruined.

The tears that temporarily stopped while she was kissing her husband were threatening to resurface. Nolan must have noticed because he reached out and gently swiped them away. "It's okay. Don't be upset with yourself over what happened to the meal. Why don't I take you to the café, instead?"

Elsie nodded, letting Nolan guide her towards the front door. "After the day I've had, I'm not in the mood to try to start over with supper."

"Nor should you have to. That's what I'm here for, to help you when things don't go the way you want them to."

The next day, Nolan returned to work, ready to find out whether John Straits was behind the theft at the train depot. Once everyone was on lunch break, Nolan took the opportunity to sneak back into the depot's office and look through the files to confirm whether or not John had received a pay raise. It didn't take long for him to establish that John hadn't received a pay raise in his short time working for the railway.

Nolan put John's file back in the cabinet, then shut the drawer. He glanced around the room, making sure everything was back in place as it was when he entered the office. Quietly, he slipped back out of the building and made his way over to the cargo hold where the men were busy prepping the items that needed to go on the next train north.

When his eyes locked on John, he wanted to confront the thief right on the spot, but Nolan knew it would be better if he did it one-on-one. If there was an audience, there was a chance they might get involved and John could get away. Or worse yet, someone could get hurt. It took every ounce of resolve he had to keep quiet about what he knew, but Nolan forced himself to do it until their work was finished.

"Can I talk with you, John, for a minute before we head home?" Nolan asked, reaching out and stopping the other man with his hand.

"Sure, but can't we just talk over at the saloon?"

"This can't wait until then," Nolan explained. "Besides, I don't want to involve anyone else."

John gave him a puzzled look as he moved towards a nearby tree and leaned against it. "Okay, so now you have me really curious. What's going on? Need some marriage advice? I can't say I'm an expert, but I'll help you if I can."

Nolan knew confronting John about the theft was going to be hard, but he didn't realize how much until he was standing there about to do it. John had always been nice to Nolan, so turning around and repaying that kindness with accusation was difficult, even if he knew it to be valid.

"It doesn't have to do with that," Nolan started, then taking a deep breath, he continued, "My wife was having lunch with your wife the other day, and Elsie commented on the new furnishings you had around the house. Your wife said you received a pay raise here at work, but I just looked into it, and that's not true."

"Your wife must be mistaken about what she thought she heard."

"No, she was quite clear about what your wife told her," Nolan stated firmly.

"Then Barbara must have gotten confused on

the matter and misspoke," John countered with a shrug. "She does that sometimes."

"I don't think so. I think that you do have extra money, but it didn't come from a pay raise. How did you get the money, John?"

"This conversation is over," John said, pushing off from the tree. "My financial affairs are none of your concern."

"They are when you're stealing from the railway," Nolan accused, stepping in front of John to block his escape route. "And that's the only way you could have possibly gotten all the extra money you have. Don't bother denying it; I looked at the time logs for when the items and deposits went missing, and you're the only person that could be behind the theft."

"You don't know what you're talking about," John yelled at Nolan as he tried to push past him. "Now get out of my way."

"No, I won't do that. You have to answer for what you've done." Nolan reached out and grabbed John by the arm. "I'm taking you down to the sheriff's office where you're going to confess to what you did, so you can stand trial."

John's eyes widened with fear as his face turned

ashen. "There's no need for that. I can save up the money, and pay it all back."

"That's not how this works. You can't be trusted now," Nolan bluntly pointed out. "There are consequences for what you did, and now you have to deal with them."

"Please, don't do this," John begged, as Nolan pulled him towards Main Street. "What will happen to Barbara? She needs me to take care of her. That's why I did all of this in the first place. She was always too good for me, and I was afraid she was going to leave me if I didn't give her all the best things in life. The need to do so only got worse when she told me she was pregnant. Now, I have two mouths to feed. I couldn't afford any of it on my pay, so I thought it wouldn't hurt to take a little bit here and there. It's not like those I stole from already didn't have a lot, so I figured it wouldn't matter in the grand scheme of things."

"It wasn't yours to take, so it did matter."

"How about this? What if I cut you in on a part of it? Think of all the nice things you could buy for Elsie? Wouldn't she love a new wardrobe and a house full of top-notch furniture? Heck, you could buy her a whole new house if you wanted. All we would have to do is take enough."

"That's not happening," Nolan stated firmly, as they passed by townsfolk, who glanced at them with confused expressions.

"You're not tempted, even a little?" John asked with hope in his voice.

Nolan shook his head. "Your thieving days are over now, and there isn't anything you can say that's going to change my mind."

"Then I'm sorry, but I have to do this." Before Nolan could even process what the other man meant, John pulled his free arm back and let it fly up and against Nolan's face. It landed with a thud against his cheek, causing Nolan to release his grip and stumble backwards.

John turned around and started running in the other direction, but Nolan didn't let him get far before he was chasing after him. "Stop, John, right now, before you make this worse."

Apparently, John either wasn't thinking straight, or he didn't care. He continued to run down Main Street, knocking people out of his way, including a couple of women, who gasped in shocked fright as he did it.

Lucky for Nolan, and unlucky for John, Nolan was a fast sprinter. It didn't take him long to catch up to the other man. Nolan reached out and yanked

John around by the shoulder. John tried to swing at him again, but this time Nolan was ready for it. He dodged the attack and followed up with two punches of his own. The blows did their job, sobering John up. "Are you done with all this foolhardiness now?" John put his hand up against the side of his face and nodded. "Good, then let's head back to the sheriff's office."

Nolan delivered John to the authorities, explaining that he was a Pinkerton agent, and how he was working the case. After he explained the evidence and detailed John's confession, he exited the sheriff's office with a sense of completion. He made his way over to the telegraph office and wired the news to his boss. A few minutes later, his boss returned a response, telling him that once everything was wrapped up in Mitchell, that Nolan was to return to Sioux Falls for his next assignment.

CHAPTER EIGHT

When Nolan arrived home, Elsie rushed up to his side, anxious to hear the details about his day. "How did it go? Were you able to find out if John Straits was behind the theft?"

Nolan nodded as he took a seat on the couch and sunk back into it. "Yes, I found the evidence to prove he didn't get a raise and decided to question him about it."

Elsie gasped as she rushed over and took a seat beside him. "Wasn't that a bit rash? He could have hurt you."

"Well, I didn't think about that until it was too late." Nolan rubbed his jaw, where a dark purple bruise was sticking out against his creamy skin. "He didn't want to go willingly to the sheriff's office."

"He hit you?" Elsie questioned with indignation in her voice. "But he was your friend."

"I guess, when you find out someone is a thief and confront them about it, a punch in the face is what you get for your troubles."

"I'm going to get you a cool rag for that welt." Elsie jumped up from the couch and scurried off towards the kitchen. She busied herself with getting a clean cloth from a drawer, wetting it, and bringing it back over to her husband. "Here, press this against it."

Nolan did as she suggested, and flinched when the rag touched his jaw. "Ouch, it's hurting a lot more than I thought it would."

"Let me help you with that. You're not getting the whole area." She took the rag from his hand and adjusted it to cover more of the rapidly growing bruise. "Tell me, you at least got a few good licks in of your own. I can't be married to a man that can't hold his own in a fight."

Nolan let out a chuckle, then grunted from the pain. "Don't make me laugh, Elsie, it hurts too much."

"I'm sorry," she whispered as she leaned closer. "I just wanted to take your mind off the pain."

"Just looking at your beautiful face does that for

me." He reached over and placed his hand on her cheek. "I couldn't wait to get home and tell you that the case is over."

Elsie bit her lip as she wondered what that meant for their relationship. Now that the case was over, did that mean their marriage was too? What would she do if Nolan no longer wanted to stay married to her? Sure, he was attracted to her and they got along well, but was that enough to make a man who enjoyed being single to one who suddenly wanted to make a temporary marriage a permanent one?

As she looked into her husband's eyes, she couldn't deny the love she felt for him, though she hadn't told him yet. Though he told her that he cared for her, she feared it wouldn't be enough to make him stay in the marriage when he had the chance to leave. After all, there was more to a relationship than attraction and friendship.

Wanting to put some distance between them, Elsie pulled away, handing the rag back to Nolan. "After all you've been through, perhaps you should rest while I cook supper."

"I couldn't think of it. Too much happened today for me to go to sleep. How about I take you out for dinner instead, before we pack to go back to Sioux Falls tomorrow."

"Tomorrow? That soon?" she questioned, still not sure she heard her husband right. "Did you say we're *both* leaving, to go back, together?"

Nolan's brows bunched together as he looked at her with perplexity. "Of course, we're going back together. We have to get our next assignment, don't we?"

Elsie folded her arms over her chest, squeezing her frame to try to steady herself. "You keep saying we, but we agreed at the beginning of this, either one of us could end our relationship after this case was concluded."

This time, Nolan's face turned from confused to angry. He sat up straight, his posture making it clear he didn't like what she was saying. "Does that mean you don't want to be married to me anymore?"

"I never said that," Elsie defended, her tone harsher then she intended.

"Then why bring it up?" he countered with frustration clear in his own voice. "I thought we were in a good place—that this arrangement was working for both of us."

Elsie didn't know what to say. She could tell he

was trying. She wasn't sure if it would be enough to make it work long-term; however, she cared too much about Nolan to just walk away. "It is, and I'm willing to continue if you are."

"Good, I'm glad to hear it."

Throughout the rest of the night, all Elsie could do was think about her future with Nolan and what it might look like. Was it possible for them to turn their arrangement into a real marriage? She hadn't hoped for love when she came out West, but now that she felt that way for her husband, she couldn't help but hope he could find it in his own heart to return it.

By the time they finished packing the last of their things, Elsie was determined to stand strong in her marriage and not give up on Nolan. She would pray and trust God to make a way for their marriage to become what they both needed.

The next morning, Elsie requested that Nolan take her out to Cara's farm so she could say goodbye to her friend. After what happened with the Straits, the other wives from the train depot refused to talk to her; all stating there was no reason to consider her a friend since they didn't even know who she was. It hurt to leave with them all mad at her, but she supposed it came as part of the job of being the wife of a Pinkerton agent.

"I'm going to miss you so, Elsie." Cara reached over and pulled her into an embrace. "You've become a good friend over a short amount of time. Please tell me you'll write and tell me of your Pinkerton adventures."

"Of course I will," she promised as she returned the hug. "I'm going to miss you too, Cara."

The children chased after them as Nolan drove their wagon towards town. They arrived at the livery, ready to check-in for the last time before catching the afternoon train back to Sioux Falls.

Once they were settled into their seats on the train, Nolan turned his attention to his wife. "I've been meaning to thank you for your help. I couldn't have closed the Mitchell case without you."

"I'm glad I could help. Your success is my success."

"I know that, and I'm realizing I'm much better with you by my side, than I am without you." Nolan reached over and patted the top of her hand that was folded in her lap. "You're a terrific partner, Elsie."

Partner. He still didn't think of her as more than a part of a business arrangement. She wanted him to see her as a wife—the woman he wanted to be with because he loved her, not because they worked well together.

Elsie pulled her hand away and leaned her head against the window with her hands underneath. "I'm feeling rather tired from everything that's happened over the last couple of days. Do you mind if I rest for a while?"

"Sure, but you don't have to lean against that cold window. You can lean on my shoulder if you like."

"It's fine," Elsie replied, purposely closing her eyes to stop the conversation. "That way if you need to get up and stretch your legs, you can. Wake me when we get there."

Even though Elsie didn't sleep the entire time they were on the train, she kept her eyes closed so she didn't have to talk with Nolan. She was worried she might say something revealing and hoped that once they got their next assignment, she could focus on that rather than on what her marriage lacked.

"There's my best agent and his wife," Agent Stansbury stated with a wide grin. "Why don't the two of you go in my office so we can discuss your next case." Elsie and Nolan followed the senior agent into the room, taking seats in front of his desk. Nolan's boss took his position behind it. "I have to commend you for doing such a thorough and quick job with the Mitchell train depot theft. When I sent you there, I honestly thought it was going to take you twice as long to get to the bottom of the situation. Because of that, I'm going to give you a case in Medora, up in the northern part of the Dakotas. It's another rail theft case. There's a possibility more than one person might be involved, including local lawmen. You'll have to be even more careful during this one, as it's in a remote part of the territory, and if the law is complicit in the theft, you won't have them to fall back on if the situation gets messy."

"When do we head to Medora?" Nolan asked, glancing over at his wife. "I was hoping to treat my wife to a dinner here in Sioux Falls since she's partial to gourmet meals."

"Take the next couple of days to relax and recuperate," Agent Stansbury ordered with a flick of his wrist towards the door. "You've both earned it. I'll set you up with a room at the hotel you stayed at last time. As for dinner, head on over to Café

Cocette and tell them that I sent you. Chef Maurice will take good care of you."

"Thank you, we appreciate that," Nolan said as they stood and exited the Pinkerton office.

"What do you think of your next assignment?" Elsie probed. "Do you think you need a wife for it to go smoothly?"

"It couldn't hurt," Nolan pointed out, as they walked down the street towards the hotel. "You make me look legitimate. Besides, I like coming home to your smiling face and supper on the table."

"I think—" before Elsie could finish her reply, she was interrupted by the familiar voice of Anne Morris.

"Elsie, is that you, dear?"

They stopped moving and turned to face the older woman. She was hurrying across the street, a smile on her face as she reached their side. "It's so good to see you. I hoped I might run into you at some point." Then glancing up at Nolan, she added, "This must be your new husband."

"Yes, Anne, this is Nolan Buckley. Nolan, this is Anne Morris, a friend I made during my train ride out here to the Dakotas."

"He's rather handsome, Elsie," Anne stated with

pride. "You did good by landing such a good-looking fellow. And he's so well-dressed, too."

Elsie noticed that Nolan's cheeks turned red under the flurry of compliments from the other woman. "Thank you, ma'am, that's quite kind of you to say."

"Don't ma'am me, young man. You're to call me Anne, just like Elsie does," she gently chastised with a twinkle in her eyes and smirk on her face. After a moment, though, she tilted her head to the side, as if she noticed something for the first time. "You know, now that I've been looking at you for a while, I think I recognize you from an article I read back in the New York newspaper. Weren't you involved in a scandal?"

Nolan shifted his stance between his feet as his eyes darted down to the ground. He shoved his hands in his pockets as he mumbled, "It didn't happen as it was reported. That story was published to ruin my reputation. I never did any of the things I was accused of."

"Well, I'm not one to judge, and if you say you didn't do it, then I believe you. Elsie has a good head on her shoulders, so if she thinks you're a good man, you must be. I have to be going, but if you're going to be in town for a while, let's grab lunch sometime."

Elsie exchanged information with Anne before they continued on their way to the hotel. She couldn't help but replay over and over in her head the conversation her husband had with the other woman. When it finally got to be too much, she blurted out, "What was Anne talking about? You've always avoided talking about what happened to you in New York to make you come out to the West. Why won't you tell me?"

Nolan let out a heavy sigh and ran his fingers through his hair in frustration. "Because I'm worried you'll think of me differently afterward."

"There's only one way to find out. Tell me, and see what I think."

They stopped just outside the hotel, but they didn't go inside. Instead, Nolan turned to face Elsie. "I told you I left New York because of a misunderstanding. The truth is, I was secretly involved with a young woman there. When her wealthy father found out, he was furious because I didn't want to marry her to protect her reputation. Because of that, he had an article printed in the newspaper that accused me of behaving inappropriately with several women, as well as a handful of prostitutes.

None of it was true. I mean, I did enjoy the company of various women, but it was always consensual and with reputable women. It didn't matter though; once the article was published, I was turned away by my friends and not allowed in the clubs and restaurants I used to frequent. Once I realized it was permanent, I decided to come out West to start over."

"That's a lot to take in. I don't know how to feel about what you just told me," Elsie confessed.

"All of that is in my past. I'm a different man now—because of you. Don't hold my poor choices against me, not after I found you. I want to spend the rest of my life with you." Nolan reached out and pulled her towards him. He leaned down and placed a kiss on her lips. She could feel the desperation behind the act, but it didn't change her own reaction to it.

Elsie let herself melt into his arms, and she sighed against his lips, enjoying the feel of kissing the man she loved. She let her hands drift up and her fingers wrap into the hair at the nape of his neck. His heart thumped in rhythm with hers, reminding her that he was just the right match for her. Once he kissed her completely breathless, she pulled back slightly and took in a couple of deep gulps of air before confirming what he needed to hear. "You're right, it doesn't matter. All that matters is our future, and that starts with our next case in Medora."

Nolan was going over the case file for his next assignment when there was a knock at the hotel room. Did Elsie forget her key? He thought he told her to take it with her when she went to the store to grab a few items for the trip, but maybe she forgot. It wouldn't be the first time.

With a small chuckle and a shake of his head, Nolan moved over to the door, saying, "Elsie, I swear if your head wasn't attached to your body, you'd forget that, too."

When he twisted the knob and pulled open the door, however, it wasn't his wife standing on the other side. Instead, his eyes settled on a towering stranger in a long, leather trench coat and a wide-brimmed hat. The man looked menacing, with a hardened stare and a pair of scars reaching from the top of his left cheek and running towards his left nostril, ending at his upper lip.

"Can I help you?" Nolan questioned with raised

eyebrows. When the stranger didn't answer, he continued as he started to shut the door. "Perhaps you should head back to the lobby and talk with the clerk. You obviously have the wrong room."

"I don't think so," the man rasped in a deep voice, as he kicked out his foot to keep the door from closing. "Nolan Buckley, I'm here to take you back to New York. There's a bounty that's been placed on you."

Nolan's throat instantly went dry. He swallowed three times, trying to force down the lump that had formed in his throat. Once he finally did, he stammered out a rebuttal. "You must be mistaken; I haven't done anything to warrant a bounty."

"Not my problem, I'm just here to collect a mighty sizable payday. Once I return you to Mr. Buchanan alive, that is." The bounty hunter roughly shoved the door open, taking Nolan by surprise. As Nolan stumbled backward, he glanced to the side, wondering if he could get to the drawer where he had put his pistol.

The bounty hunter must have noticed where his eyes went because he darted towards the dresser to block his path. "Oh no you don't. I heard you got a job as a Pinkerton, and agents always have a gun stashed in their domicile."

Nolan clenched his jaw in frustration. This fellow was good at his job, which was bad for Nolan. His chances of outsmarting him and getting away were decreasing by every second. Plus, if he managed to escape by some miracle and went on the run again, it would mean the end of his relationship with Elsie. The only way to salvage the life he built for himself in the Dakotas would be to eliminate the bounty hunter and find a way to get the bounty removed once he did.

With quick precision, Nolan struck out towards the other man, but he must have anticipated what Nolan was going to do. The bounty hunter dodged the punch, then pulled out his holstered gun. "That's enough, Mr. Buckley; the bounty is for you to be alive, but you don't want to press my resolve. I'm sure I could negotiate with Mr. Buchanan to pay me half if I bring your head back to him."

Nolan froze, his eyes widening with fear. He could tell from the bounty hunter's disposition, he had no problem carrying through on his threat. Nolan's only option was to go along with him for now, and hope an opportunity to escape would present itself. Once he did, he could make his way back to Elsie and explain what happened. If her feelings for him were half as strong as how he felt about her, maybe she would be willing to go on the run with him. Either way, he owed it to her to not just disappear without trying to let her know why.

As the bounty hunter escorted him out of the hotel with a barrel of a gun pressed against his back, Nolan decided it was important to keep the other man distracted by talking to him. "Where are you taking me? To the sheriff's office?"

The other man snorted. "No, this bounty isn't necessarily above board. I won't be involving any lawmen. We're headed straight to the train station."

This was Nolan's answer to how he might get out of this. The bounty hunter didn't want to draw attention because it could cause the authorities to get involved. All he had to do was cause a big enough scene right when they passed by the sheriff's office on the way to the train depot.

"You know, it says a lot about a person's integrity when he's willing to trade another man's life for a paycheck."

"Everyone's got to make a living," the bounty hunter retorted back with a shrug.

"True, but not everyone has to do it by being a snollygoster."

The bounty hunter stopped moving, his eyes

narrowing into slits as he snarled out, "What did you just call me?"

"You heard me; you're a no-good, sneaky pettifogger," Nolan yelled at the other man as he spun around to face him, hoping that he would fight Nolan rather than shoot him.

He got his wish. The bounty hunter swung his free arm out, connecting with Nolan's right eye. The pain of it was staggering, and he wouldn't be surprised if it didn't break the eye socket. He forced himself to push through the pain and throw a punch of his own. The two men continued to exchange blows back and forth, causing a crowd to form around them. Just when Nolan didn't think he could take anymore, there was a loud shout from amongst the townsfolk. "Stop this, right now."

Nolan wanted to oblige, but the bounty hunter wasn't having any of it. He continued the fight, bent on knocking Nolan out flat on his back.

"Enough." A hand stretched out and grabbed Nolan by the shoulder. "You're both coming with us."

Nolan noticed that three men with shiny silver badges on their chest came into view. Two of the men were subduing the bounty hunter by handcuffing him.

"He wasn't listening to us, so we made him." The average-looking man with a stern face inspected Nolan as if sizing up what he was made of. "Do we need to do the same with you?"

Nolan shook his head. "I was hoping you would show up."

"You might be the first brawler that ever wanted the sheriff to intervene."

"You're the lesser of two problems. I could either take my chances with you or end up being carted across the country to be handed over to a bad man, who plans to kill me."

"Do you deserve it?" the sheriff asked bluntly.

Before he could answer, he heard Elsie's sweet voice cry out to him. "Nolan, what on earth is going on?"

"It's nothing, Elsie."

She tried to push close to him, but the sheriff stopped her. "Ma'am you need to stay back. This man is under arrest."

"That man is my husband," Elsie shouted at the sheriff, "and he hasn't done anything to deserve what you're doing to him."

"It's okay, I'll have it all sorted out in no time," Nolan promised, shouting over his shoulder as he was carted off. The lawmen guided the brawlers over to the jail inside the sheriff's office.

Once there, they tossed them both in side-by-side cells. Nolan was thankful that a set of bars separated him from the bounty hunter, but as another looming figure stepped out of the shadows, Nolan realized he might have traded one problem for another.

CHAPTER NINE

A chill of apprehension shot up Elsie's back as she walked into the Sioux Falls Sheriff's office. It took more convincing than she anticipated to get them to let her in the back. By the time she did, Nolan was already sitting on a bench in the corner of the cell, watching everything around him in a way that made it clear he was worried.

Elsie rushed up to the bars, wrapping her hand around them as she peered through them at her husband. "Are you all right? Did they hurt you?"

He shook his head. "I'm fine, Elsie. Just sore from having my face punched during two different fights over the last couple of days."

"What happened? Why were you in a fight this time?"

"My past caught up to me. I hoped to outrun it, but it seems that what I left behind festered and became something even worse during my absence. The father of the woman whose reputation I ruined, placed a private bounty on my head. The man in the other cell came to collect on that bounty, and I ended up starting a fight so he couldn't force me to leave town with him."

"But once we get out of these jail cells, I'm coming right after you again. There's nowhere you can hide, Mr. Buckley," the bounty hunter threatened from the wall he was leaning against.

Nolan glanced over at the bounty hunter, a wary look on his face. He lowered his voice as he continued to talk to Elsie. "I don't know what I'm going to do, Elsie. Now that I have a bounty on my head, I'm never going to be safe again. When I started that fight, I figured it would be better to end up in here, so I could at least have a chance to see you again and explain what happened." Nolan reached out and gripped her hands with his. He pressed his face against the bars, placing a tender kiss on her forehead. "I'm really sorry about all of this, Elsie. My past bad choices have made a real mess of things. I'll understand if you walk away from me."

"If you do, you should know there are plenty of other options around here." A tall, dark-haired man, wearing a pair of dark pants and equally black shirt, stepped out of the shadows of the cell and leaned against the bars; a sly, flirtatious grin etched across his face. He was staring at her in a way that made her uncomfortable. It was as if his pale gray eyes could see right through her, and she didn't like it.

Elsie's own face scrunched up with indignation. "I don't see how you can offer anyone, anything, from behind those bars. You're in no better position than my husband."

"Oh this," the tall man dismissed his precarious situation with a nonchalant shrug. "This is temporary. The sheriff in Mitchell transferred me here when I became too much to handle. I won't be here long, though. I've got friends in high places."

"That's what everyone says when they land themselves in jail," the deputy stated snidely from his desk across the room.

"But in my case, it happens to be the truth," the tall man countered with a deep voice, thick with arrogance.

"Riker, you wouldn't know the truth if it bit you on your…" the deputy's eyes moved over to Elsie, prompting him not to finish his sentence. "Pardon me, ma'am, but that degenerate really irritates me. I can't wait until the marshals arrive, and he officially is no longer my problem."

"Believe me, I can't wait to get out of here and be rid of you, too, deputy, but it won't be by the hand of marshals. My friends will be showing up shortly to secure my immediate release."

"Keep dreaming, Riker. You've been saying that for days now."

Riker turned his attention back to Elsie, his flirtatious smile returning. "As for you, darlin', I could take really good care of you, and teach you a couple of useful skills along the way. Everyone needs a good protector, and I'm quite good at protecting a damsel in distress."

"Even if you weren't behind these bars, and I wasn't a married woman, I would never associate with the likes of you. It's clear from your conduct over the past couple of minutes, you're a scoundrel of the highest order."

"I wouldn't deny that," Riker stated with a chuckle. "However, that's never stopped a woman from taking up with me though. I'm sure I could convince you to do the same."

"Leave my wife alone," Nolan growled out as he let go of the bars and turned to face the other man.

"Or what? You're going to make me," Riker challenged with a raised eyebrow, as if daring him to do it. He moved towards Nolan, who didn't back down.

"If I have to I will. I won't have anyone talking to my wife the way you have been."

Just when Elsie was certain the men were going to start swinging their fists, there was a commotion towards the front of the sheriff's office, drawing everyone's attention. The deputy jumped up and rushed through the door that separated the jail from the lobby. There was a bunch of loud voices, arguing heatedly, and then another man—Elsie recognized him from earlier as the sheriff—came back through the door. He marched over to the desk and pulled out a set of keys, then moved over to the cell that Nolan and Riker were in, an angry look on his face. "Let's go, Riker. It seems you weren't lying about having some powerful friends."

Riker picked up his hat from the nearby cot, slipped it onto his head as he strode out from the cell. "Thank you, Sheriff, for the fond farewell."

"Shut your mouth, Riker. I've had all I can

stomach of you. I may have to release you, but it doesn't mean I have to do it without any bumps or bruises along the way."

Riker pranced out of the jail, cocky and proud that his prediction came true. On his way out of the building, she could hear him telling off the deputies in a smug voice.

Elsie suddenly realized Riker might be the answer to her prayers. She gestured for Nolan to come to the bars, then leaned into them, placing a kiss on his lips. "I think I might have found a way to get you out of all this. I have to go right now."

"Don't do anything reckless," Nolan pleaded to her departing figure. "I don't want you to get into trouble because of me."

Once outside the sheriff's office, Elsie rushed after Riker. "Mister, mister, can I speak with you for a moment?"

Riker stopped in his tracks, turning around to face her, a seductive smile instantly curling his lips up. "Change your mind, darlin'?"

"No, not on anything you offered; however, I was wondering if you might be willing to ask those friends of yours to help out my husband."

"Now, why on earth would I do that? I don't just

go around calling in favors for anyone, darlin'. What are you willing to do for me in exchange?"

Elsie's eyes widened with shock, disgusted by the implication behind the salacious man's words. "I don't have anything to offer you, Mr. Riker."

"It's just Riker, and of course you do, Elsie." He reached out and let his hand brush along her arm, causing her skin to prickle under his touch. "You have plenty to offer me if you want to."

Elsie jerked away and backed up, giving him a withering glare. "You're mistaken; that's not why I came after you."

"Isn't it though? How much do you love your husband?"

Elsie pressed her lips together as she thought about that answer. "More than you could ever fathom."

"Then what are you willing to do to secure his freedom?"

"No matter how much I want to save him, I could never betray him by giving you what you want. I was wrong to come after you. You're just as crooked as I first thought." Elsie spun around and ran off in the opposite direction, discouraged that she had no idea how she was going to help her husband.

What was she going to do now? Nolan was in real danger of being carted off to New York where he could be killed. She needed to figure out a way to keep that from happening. There had to be something she could do.

Agent Stansbury. Couldn't he help them? Nolan was an excellent agent, and they spent a lot of time and money training him. There was no way he wanted to lose him if he could avoid it.

Elsie found herself heading towards the Pinkerton agency office. She hurried inside, knowing that time was of the essence because she had no idea how long before they released Nolan.

"I need to speak with Agent Stansbury," Elsie demanded. "It's urgent."

The secretary escorted her inside as Agent Stansbury started to stand to his feet to greet Elsie.

"There's no need for that," Elsie said, gesturing for him to remain seated. She perched on the edge of a chair across from him and immediately went into an explanation of the situation.

"What is it that you want me to do exactly, Mrs. Buckley?"

"I want you to help secure the safe release of my husband, and help make it so that the bounty on his head goes away."

"That's a lot of work for me and this agency. Part of me wonders if it would be better for me to just let Nolan handle his own mess, and we move on with our other agents. I don't see how this would benefit the agency enough to warrant the investment."

Elsie knew the only way to save Nolan, was to make sure Agent Stansbury was willing to help them. She needed to offer him something to sweeten the deal. "I read in the newspaper that your agency is wanting female agents. What if I agree to become one, on my own?"

"I want to be clear, Mrs. Buckley; what are you offering?"

Elsie swallowed the lump in her throat, knowing that she might have to give up the man she loved in order to save him. It would be worth it though if it meant he was safe. "If you help Nolan, I will work for you as an independent agent. You can assign me anywhere, and I'll go without a complaint."

"Let me see what I can do."

When the cell door opened and Nolan walked out of the jail, he couldn't help but feel the relief that flooded him. Elsie was waiting on the other side, along with Agent Stansbury. At first, Nolan was a little surprised to see his boss there, but then he realized Elsie must have made the smart decision to go to him and ask him for help.

"Thank you for doing this," Nolan said to both of them as they exited the sheriff's office. "That was the longest day of my life."

"Why don't I take you back to the hotel where you can rest," Elsie offered. "You must be exhausted."

"How did you get me out of there?" Nolan asked his boss.

"The agency has a lot of influence in Sioux Falls. We've helped the sheriff with several cases. I explained that you're one of my agents and that the situation with the bounty hunter was a misunderstanding."

"I appreciate you doing that for me."

"It wasn't me, as much as your wife. She convinced me to do it. She cares a great deal about you, Mr. Buckley. You should count yourself lucky. She even offered to become an independent agent to secure your release and to have me deal with your bounty issue."

"You did all that for me?" Nolan asked his wife with appreciation. "That means so much."

"Of course I did, you're my husband."

They arrived in front of the hotel and Agent Stansbury explained what would happen next. "You'll leave for your next assignment tomorrow under your new aliases. In the meantime, I'll fabricate evidence that Nolan met with the end of a hangman's noose in a remote part of the Dakotas. I'll make sure that the information makes it back to Mr. Buchanan through one of the undercover Pinkerton agents back East."

"Thank you, I appreciate it."

As they made their way back to their hotel room, Nolan decided to finally ask Elsie about her deal with his boss. "Did you mean it?"

"Mean what?" Elsie asked with confusion as she opened the door with the key.

"Are you going to become an independent agent? Are you leaving me?"

Elsie's brows bunched together as she shook her head. "No, I offered to save you, but Agent Stansbury thinks we're better together as a team. He does want you to train me as an agent during our next job, but that's it."

"What does that mean for us, our relationship?"

Nolan probed further, hoping Elsie would confirm she had romantic feelings for him like he did for her.

"I guess that means you're stuck with me," she stated with a small awkward laugh.

"That's good, because I can't imagine my life without you in it," Nolan confessed. "I'm so glad that you aren't leaving me. I hope you'll give me the chance to make this marriage real. I love you, Elsie. I want to start a family with you and spend the rest of my life with you." He leaned forward and kissed her passionately on the lips, hoping she could feel the sincere love behind the gesture.

Elsie leaned back, her face flush from his kisses. "I love you too, Nolan. I've loved you for a long time now, but I was afraid you didn't feel the same way about me."

"How could I not love you, Elsie? You're amazing. You light up my life. Every moment I spend with you is better than the last." He lifted her up into his arms, spinning her around and around until they both fell back onto the bed. "I'm so glad that my boss was smart enough to place an advert in the newspaper and that you were desperate enough to answer it. You being my mail-order bride was the best thing that ever happened to me."

Elsie reached out and placed her hand on the side of his face. "I feel the same way. I'm so glad that you're my husband, and I get to spend the rest of my life with you. I never knew I could be this happy. I couldn't ask for anything more."

If you want to find out what finally happens to Riker, read his story in <u>Mail Order Miscast.</u>

SNEAK PEAK OF MAIL ORDER MISCAST

Charleston, West Virginia 1885

"You can't be genuine about this, Father," Vivian Humble gasped as her mouth dropped open and stared at her father with disbelief. "How can you possibly expect me to marry Phillip Anderson?"

"You'll see in time, Vivie, that this is the best for you," her aging father promised as he sat behind his antique wooden desk in his study. "Phillip has the means to take care of you the way you're accustomed to. When I pass, your brother will inherit everything, so you need to marry well. Phillip's always had a soft spot where you're concerned, and I wasn't surprised when he proposed the idea of marriage. He's been heartbroken since his wife passed away a year ago. They never had children, so you could give him something."

Vivian shook with anger, the frustration and rage bubbling up uncontrollably. Of all the preposterous notions, she couldn't believe that her father's solution to her status as a spinster was this. "So, if I am to understand you correctly, Father, you want me to marry your business partner—who is nearly as old as you are—because he has money and wants children. You think me willing to exchange one for the other, like I'm a broodmare being sold to the highest bidder?"

"Be reasonable, Vivie; you're overreacting. You know Father has your best interest in mind," her brother, Jonathan, coaxed. He placed his hand on her shoulder, squeezing as he flashed her a sympathetic smile.

"What does Mother have to say about this? I don't see her here, which makes me wonder if she objects to this as much as I do," Vivian questioned, hoping the matriarch of the family would be an ally for her cause.

"Your mother has deferred to my good judgment on the matter. We've indulged you for far too long. Your pickiness over a husband has cost you countless opportunities. We will not allow you to squander this one," her father stated firmly.

Never would she have guessed her desire to hold out for love would result in her ending up marrying the likes of Phillip Anderson. He was just as shrewd as he was manipulative, setting his eyes on her as soon as his wife had died. Vivian had rebuffed his advances hoping his interest with her would soon pass. Apparently, that hadn't happened. Instead, he had played on her father's good nature to get what he wanted, and that didn't mean she had to go along with it though. She had one last bit of information she hoped would convince her father that Mr. Anderson would be a horrible match for her.

"What about the rumors, Father? You've had to have heard he was spotted all over town with numerous women."

"He's grieving, Vivie. If he sought comfort after his wife's death, you can't fault him for that," her father defended.

"If his promiscuous ways were only since his wife's death, that would be one thing. His questionable morality, however, has been whispered about for far longer than that. He spends time with women of ill-repute, Father. How could you want me to marry a man that carries on in such a fashion?" Vivian questioned, as she shook her dark brown hair with disgust.

"You shouldn't repeat such baseless allegations, Vivie," her father chastised with a disapproving frown, emphasizing the deep-set wrinkles around his mouth. "Phillip is a decent man and promises to take good care of you. I've made my decision, and you'll marry him at the end of the month."

Vivian's mouth went dry, realizing that no matter what she said, her father had made up his mind. He was determined to see her married to his business partner. It didn't matter how much money they made with their coal mine, Vivian couldn't imagine being married to a reprobate like Phillip Anderson.

"I'm not feeling very well. I think I need some fresh air," she mumbled as she spun around and exited the study without waiting for a dismissal. If she stayed there one more moment longer, she would have picked up the nearest antique bauble and thrown it across the room. To avoid dealing with her feelings over the matter, there was only one thing that would do the trick. Vivian marched to her room to grab her reticule and parasol, determined to push the awful news far from her mind.

"A shopping trip is in order, Constance," Vivian declared to her maid as she busied herself with getting ready for her outing. "We both know I do my best thinking when I'm picking out a new dress and a matching hat."

"What's the occasion, dear?" her mother inquired as she glided into her suite of rooms. "I know you often think my tastes border on gaudy, but this is a big moment in your life. Please tell me that you weren't thinking of excluding your mother from picking out your wedding gown?"

"Not at all, Mother, since I'm not planning on getting married any time soon, least of all to Phillip Anderson." Vivian slammed down her brush and glared at her mother in the mirror of her vanity.

"Come now, Vivie, don't be so contrary," her mother sighed as she let herself sink into the couch beside the window, the back of her hand pressed against her forehead as if she were about to faint. Leave it to her mother to always be dramatic. "You knew this day would come eventually. All women must marry at some point, and you've managed to wait far longer than most. It's your job to make the best of the match your father has made for you."

"I will do no such thing," Vivian objected, jumping up from her seat. "He's repugnant, Mother. Why would you want your only daughter to marry someone like that?"

Her mother tilted her head toward her, shrugging, "It could be worse; you could be marrying someone who is ugly, or worse, poor." The disdain in her mother's voice made it clear that the lack of a full pocket and bank account deemed a person completely unacceptable.

"Mother, I don't expect you to understand. You and I have entirely different opinions on what makes a good match. I want a husband who loves me and only me."

"Dear, it's about time you gave up such silly notions as marrying for love." Her mother sat up and waved her hands in the air as if she were swatting away the ridiculous idea. "Truthfully, one has little to do with the other. Security, status, legacy, they're the cornerstones of a lasting union. You'll understand that in time."

"I'm not like you, Mother. I can't imagine looking the other way while my husband runs around with other women." As soon as she said the words, Vivian regretted it. The hurt in her mother's eyes only lasted a few flickering seconds, but long enough to make Vivian blush with embarrassment. "I shouldn't have said that. I'm sorry, Mother."

"It doesn't matter. You should take a lesson from me and figure out a way to make peace with your lot in life. There is no way around it. You're marrying the man your father picked out for you."

On her short carriage ride into the shopping district of town, Vivian mulled over her mother's words. Was she right? Did Vivian need to resign herself to the fact that she was going to be tied to an awful man for the rest of her life? She didn't see what other choice she had in the matter, but in her heart of hearts, she couldn't quite convince herself to give up on the possibility of figuring out a way to get free from the situation.

Vivian spent the rest of the afternoon shuffling between the various stores that littered the cobblestone streets. She visited the hat shop, the shoemakers, the perfumery, and even picked up a treat at the bakery. Her final stop for the day was the dress shop, saving the best for the end. As soon as she entered the establishment, the last bit of tension she'd been carrying around all day melted away. She drifted through the store, her fingers lingering here and there on the plush velvets and soft satins as she scanned the store for the perfect dress. An emerald green, velvet gown drew her attention. Instantly, she knew it would enhance the color of her hazel eyes, pulling out the flecks of green within them.

"This is the one, Constance. I have to have it." Vivian reached out to lift the gown off the rack, but another hand beat her to it.

"Oh, pardon me," a young woman with bright red hair stammered with embarrassment. "I didn't know you were looking at the same dress."

"You seem to have gotten to the gown first," Vivian admitted, trying to hide the disappointment that she would lose out on wearing the one-of-a-kind creation.

"I'd let you have it if it didn't matter so much that I make a good first impression when I reach Colorado. My future husband sent me money to buy a couple of dresses, and I want to make sure he's happy with my selections when I arrive."

"Why in heavens would you need to make a first impression?" Vivian asked with confusion. "You're set to marry the man. Surely, the task of getting to know one another is already accomplished."

The young woman shrugged, her cheeks turning even redder under the scrutiny. "Not when you're a mail-order bride, as I am," the redhead confessed. "I won't meet my groom until the day I arrive to marry him."

What on earth was a mail-order bride? Vivian had never heard of such a thing. It sounded preposterous, yet part of her wondered if such arrangements really took place. Could this possibly be a solution for her?

Vivian wanted to question the young woman about her situation, but she had to do it without an audience. She glanced over at her maid, knowing she had to get rid of the other woman if she wanted any chance of finding out the details without raising suspicion.

"Constance, please return to the milliners. I believe I left my favorite handkerchief there while I was trying on hats."

"Yes, ma'am, I'll be back as soon as I can," the gray-haired servant said with a nod as she scurried out of the store.

Once she was certain Constance was gone, Vivian returned her attention to the redhead. "Now that we're free from distractions, tell me all about how you became a mail order bride."

Grab your copy of <u>Mail Order Miscast</u>.

SNEAK PEAK OF MAIL ORDER MIRANDA

Early Spring of 1881
Lake Hope, Pennsylvania

The baby's earsplitting cries echoed down the hall, causing Miranda Barton to cover her head with a pillow. Nearly every night for the past six months, her niece, Eleanor, woke bellowing at one in the morning. Her precise timing would be commendable if it wasn't so exasperating.

"Please, Elle, just for one night, stop crying," Miranda mumbled into the mattress of her bed. "I just need one good night's sleep before I head to Texas in two days."

As if to show who was in charge of the house, Eleanor's cries increased both in tempo and shrillness.

Miranda threw the pillow off her head and rolled over, swinging her legs over the side of the bed. She might as well check on her sister, Elizabeth, who would no doubt be tending the baby while her husband, Albert, was fast asleep. It always stunned her how that man could sleep so soundly through such a grating nightly occurrence.

After slipping on her robe, Miranda padded down the hallway until she reached the nursery. She pushed the door open and observed from the threshold. Elizabeth was in the rocking chair, gently moving it back and forth in an effort to soothe the baby. Eleanor wasn't having any of it though. Her tiny pink face scrunched up in a wretched scowl before another bloodcurdling scream projected from her mouth.

"Did you try offering her some bread with a little brandy on it?" Miranda inquired, moving further into the room. "Jane said it could help."

"Yes, I tried it, and Elle promptly spit it out. She only cried harder afterward, making it that much more difficult to calm her down. Jane might be the pastor's wife, but she isn't an expert on everything, though she seems to think so," Elizabeth stated sarcastically with a shake of her head. "I don't know how much more of this I can take, Miranda. What if Eleanor never outgrows this behavior?"

"Here, give her to me for a bit." Miranda reached out to take her niece. "You look as though you might break down and weep at any moment." Miranda placed Eleanor's stomach against her own chest and gently patted her back as she paced the floor. Within a few minutes, the motion did its trick and her niece drifted off to sleep.

"How did you do that?" Elizabeth marveled, with a hint of envy in her voice. "It never ceases to amaze me how good you are with her. I don't know what I'm going to do without you when you leave in two days."

"It's all in the walk," Miranda said, continuing to pace back and forth to make sure Eleanor didn't wake up. "You just need to keep a steady cadence, and pat her back at the same time."

Elizabeth shook her head. "You make it sound so easy, but I've tried doing exactly that. It's not what you do, or even how you do it. It's you, Miranda; you have a gift when it comes to children. They bond with you in a way that is very special."

Miranda hoped her sister was right. She was

going to need that special gift if she was going to be capable of taking on the job of being a mother to twin almost three-year-old boys. When she saw Cade Tanner's advert for a mail order bride in the *Matrimonial Times*, she nearly passed it up when it mentioned the children. She hadn't been sure if she was interested in having an instant family, but when all the other adverts were placed by morally bankrupt scoundrels or old men looking for a young wife, she decided children might be the least of her problems.

Elizabeth insisted that she didn't need to leave, but Miranda didn't want to be a burden anymore. Her sister and her husband were barely surviving on his income as a constable. Miranda supposed she could have tried to get a job herself, but with no education or experience to speak of, reputable jobs for a woman were scarce.

"You'll be fine," Miranda encouraged, as she placed Eleanor in her crib. "You're a great mother. Eleanor will get through this, and soon all her fussiness will be a distant memory."

"I hope you're right, but that doesn't change the fact I'm going to miss you so much when you leave."

"I'll miss you, too, but you can come visit any time."

"I'd like that," Elizabeth stood up and squeezed her sister's hand. "I'll pray for safe travels for you. It's a long train ride to Texas."

Tomorrow, Miranda would be setting off for her new life in Rockwood Springs. All of her belongings were packed and ready for the trip. She had her ticket and traveling money her future husband had wired to her safely tucked in her tapestry bag.

A nervous excitement was in the pit of her stomach as she held Eleanor in her arms. Gently, she patted the infant's back just the way she liked it. Once Elizabeth and Albert returned from the market, they would help her with her final arrangements before departure. In no time at all, she was going to be barreling down the rails heading to Cade and his sons.

"I'm going to miss you, Elle, but this is going to be better for everyone," Miranda whispered in her niece's ear. She didn't like the idea of leaving her behind, but it had to be this way. "I know I'm a burden to your parents, and that isn't fair. I need to find a way to make a life for myself. Cade and his boys need me, and I can make a life with them. I hope one day you'll be able to come and visit me." She turned her face and gently kissed the baby's cheek, trying to repress the tears that were forming in the corners of her eyes.

There was a knock at the door, and Miranda moved from the parlor into the entry hall of the house. Maybe it was some of the women from church coming to say goodbye. Most of them hadn't been the most supportive in the beginning when she told them her plans to be a mail order bride, but there were still a few that might come to wish her farewell.

She opened the door and on the other side stood men wearing dark blue constable uniforms. She recognized both men from her sister's wedding as well as from church. What put her on edge was they both had a look in their eyes that didn't bode well for why they were there.

"Good morning, Miss Barton, can we come in?" the taller of the men asked politely.

She nodded, stepping back to let them enter. "Please, follow me into the parlor."

"Miss Barton, you might want to sit down for what we need to tell you," the shorter, portly man said with a sad smile. "This is going to be difficult to hear."

Miranda's stomach tightened with dread. "What is it?"

"There was a robbery at the market today. The owner of one of the stores pulled a gun to defend himself, but the thieves shot back. Unfortunately, your sister and Albert were caught in the crossfire."

"Are they going to be all right? Are they at the hospital?" Miranda inquired, already figuring out in her head who she would ask to watch Eleanor while she went to tend to her family. She'd have to write her future husband, of course, and explain she would be delayed for a few days, possibly weeks, but hopefully he would understand.

"I'm sorry to say, Miss Barton, neither of them survived. Their wounds were too severe," the taller constable informed her with a sympathetic look.

Miranda's whole body started to shake, her knees were suddenly weak, and the room was spinning out of control.

"Miss Barton, here, let me help you. You don't want to drop the baby," the shorter constable shouted as he came up beside her and guided her onto the sofa nearby.

The baby, what was going to happen to

Eleanor? She was an orphan now, just like Miranda. She never hoped to share such a heartbreaking connection with her niece.

"Can we get someone for you, Miss Barton? Do you have any family nearby?" the shorter constable offered.

She shook her head, tears falling down her cheeks in rapid succession. "My sister was all the family I had left, she and my niece. What is to become of the baby?"

"Albert didn't have any family left either, did he?" the taller constable asked.

She shook her head, and forced herself to swallow the lump in her throat so she could answer. "We were all orphans. We often lamented that it was what bound us all together."

"I suppose you would be charged with taking care of her then, if you're willing," the taller man explained. "You're the only family she has left."

Miranda looked down at her sleeping niece. Eleanor was her responsibility now. She needed to do whatever it would take to take care of her. Her protective instincts kicked in. She wasn't sure what she was going to do, but she needed help.

"Can you fetch Pastor Phillips and his wife for me?" she inquired.

The taller constable nodded, then leaned over and whispered to the other man, who a couple of moments later, scurried off towards the front door.

"I can stay with you until they arrive if you'd like," he offered.

She nodded, the constable accepting the gesture as a sign that he could take a seat in the nearby chair.

They sat in silence while they waited, neither of them having any words that could make the situation more palatable. Eleanor started to stir, causing Miranda to shift in her seat. She hoped the baby couldn't sense the tension in her body. The last thing she needed was for her niece to wake up and start crying.

A half hour later, the constable returned with the middle-aged pastor and his wife. It was clear from the expressions on their faces that the constable already told them what had happened.

"Oh my, dear, I'm so sorry," Jane stated in a soothing tone as she took a seat next to Miranda on the couch. "We're here for you, whatever you need."

"Thank you," she pushed out through the lump in her throat, trying to respond the way she was raised to do.

"Do you want us to take a letter to the post office to be sent to that man you were planning to marry in Texas? I'm assuming that absurd idea isn't happening now," Jane stated in a way that made it clear she didn't approve.

Miranda hadn't thought about Cade since she found out about her sister and Albert's deaths. It didn't mean that she didn't want to follow through with her commitment, because she did. She just wasn't sure how she could do that now that she had Eleanor to consider.

"Jane, I can handle that on my own. What I need help with is planning the funeral. I don't know the first thing about it since Elizabeth took care of it for our parents."

"I can handle all of that in the next couple of days," Pastor Phillips offered.

"No, tonight," Miranda stated firmly. "I can use the little bit of money my sister had saved up for the funeral but it has to be done tonight."

"Why is that, dear?" Jane asked with confusion. "That's awfully quick."

"Because, I have a train ticket I need to use tomorrow. I need all of this settled before I go."

Jane's eyes grew round with shock. "You're not seriously thinking of still going to Texas, are you?"

"I don't have much choice, Jane. I know my sister and Albert were already in a dire financial situation. It's why I was leaving in the first place, so I wouldn't be a burden on them anymore. The funeral will take up what little savings they had, so afterward, I have to go to Texas and marry Cade Tanner."

If Miranda had the money, she would've sent a telegram to Cade and told him about her new unexpected circumstances. She didn't have enough money, however, to both bury Elizabeth and Albert and send a telegram, nor the time to send a letter and wait for his reply. She also couldn't find it in herself to beg others to help take care of her and Eleanor. Everyone was having a difficult time providing for their own families since the mill burned down six months prior. It was the major source of income for the town.

"At the very least, then, you should leave Eleanor with us," Jane suggested. "Such a long trip across the country would be difficult on a baby. Besides, you have no idea what's waiting for you at the end of it. Would your intended even want another, unexpected mouth to feed?"

Miranda worried about that, too. Would Cade be upset if she arrived with a baby in her arms?

He'd placed an advert for a mail order bride, not a mail order baby. Would he turn them both out once she got there?

Her mind flashed to the last letter she received from him.

I will not lie to you, Miranda. My heart still aches for my dearly departed wife. It is wounded and needs time to heal. I know; however, my children do not have the luxury of waiting while that happens. They need a mother now.

I love children, and know that I have the capacity to love as many as the Lord is willing to bless us with through our marriage. I vow to you I will be a kind and considerate husband, just as I am a father.

She had to believe from the promises he made in his letter, that if she brought Eleanor with her, he would take her in as his own.

Grab your copy of <u>Mail Order Miranda.</u>

ALSO BY JENNIFER BRANSON/JENNA BRANDT

Most Books are Free in Kindle Unlimited

JENNIFER BRANSON'S HISTORICAL ROMANCE

Mail Order Mix-Up Series

~sweet historical romance~

Mail order bride books about women venturing out West to make new lives for themselves. What happens when they decide to take a chance on love along the way?

Mail Order Misfit

Mail Order Misstep

Mail Order Miscast

Mail Order Misaim

Mail Order Misplay

Mail Order Mister

Mail Order Mishap

MOMU Box Set

Brides of Persimmon Pass Series

~sweet historical romance~

Meet the Brides of Persimmon Pass. Strong, brave women with hearts of gold each in need of a man to survive in the Old West. Enter the cowboys, ranchers, & deputies ready to take on the challenge of the rural town & the women in it.

Counting on the Cowboy

Gambling on the Gentleman

Doting on the Deputy

Relying on the Rancher

Flipping on the Farmer

Banking on the Businessman

The Civil War Brides Trilogy

~sweet historical romance~

During the bloodiest conflict on American soil, two families struggle in the South to not only survive but to thrive.

Saved by Faith

Freed by Hope

Healed by Grace

CWB Box Set

Second Chance Brides of the Old West

~sweet historical romance~

Widows, single moms, matchmakers, and love triangles fill the pages of this series. Each woman finds her own path to happiness.

Discreetly Matched

June's Remedy

Becca's Lost Love

Hard to Please

The Lawkeepers

~sweet historical romantic suspense~

A multi-author series alternating between historical westerns and contemporary westerns featuring law enforcement heroes that span multiple agencies and generations. Join bestselling author Jenna Brandt and many others as they weave captivating, sweet and inspirational stories of romance and suspense between the lawkeepers — and the women who love them. The Lawkeepers is a world like no other; a world where lawkeepers and heroes are honored with unforgettable stories, characters, and love.

Jennifer's Lawkeeper books:

Historical

Lawfully Loved-Texas Sheriff

Lawfully Wanted-Bounty Hunter

Lawfully Forgiven-Texas Ranger

Lawfully Avenged-US Marshal

Lawfully Covert-Spies

Lawfully Historical Box Set

Widows, Brides, and Secret Babies

~sweet historical romance~

Mail order bride stories with a twist. What happens when a bride arrives pregnant or with a secret child?

Mail Order Miranda

Mail Order Miriam

Secret Baby Dilemma

~sweet historical romance~

Each mail order bride arrives with a baby or pregnant, and the prospective groom doesn't know until her arrival.

Mail Order Madeline

JENNA BRANDT'S CONTEMPORARY ROMANCE

First Responders of Faith Valley

~sweet romantic suspense~

Fall in love with a small Texas town filled with heroes willing to put their lives on the line for others. Brothers wearing the same badge, cousins fighting the same fire, paramedics saving citizens, all while trying to find their way to the perfect soulmate.

Saving His Reputation

(Free with Newsletter sign-up)

Arresting Her Heart

Sparking A Romance

Reviving Their Love

Guarding Her Secret

Rescuing Their Date

Mending A Broken Past

Disaster City Search and Rescue

~sweet romantic suspense~

Step into the world of Disaster City Search and Rescue, where officers, firefighters, military, and medics, train and work alongside each other with the dogs they love, to do the most dangerous job of all — help lost and injured victims find their way home.

The Girlfriend Rescue

The Billionaire Rescue

The Wedding Rescue

(Free with Newsletter sign-up)

The Movie Star Rescue

The Best Friend Rescue

The Ex-Wife Rescue

The Cowgirl Rescue

The Single Mom Rescue

The Pop Singer Rescue

The Army Ranger Rescue

The Boss's Baby Rescue

The Patriot Rescue

The Forgetful Princess Rescue

The Holiday Rescue

The Mistaken Identity Rescue

The Bombshell Rescue

The High Stakes Rescue

The Dark Water Rescue

The Thanksgiving Rescue

Hero Search and Rescue

~sweet romantic comedy with a dash of suspense~

Come visit the small town of Hero, Texas where the neighbors or nosy, the B&B is supposedly haunted, and the new search and rescue academy's the talk of the town.

Small Town Start

Small Town Splurge

Small Town Smarty

Small Town Style

Wild Animal Protection Agency

~sweet romantic suspense~

Come be apart of the adventure, danger, and heartfelt moments with the Wild Animal Protection Agency, where brave men and women work alongside each other all over the world, to do the most risky job of all — rescue injured and endangered wild animals.

Rescue Agent for Dana

Rescue Agent for Sarah

Rescue Agent for Kylie

Rescue Agent for Josette

Rescue Agent for Margo

Rescue Agent for Penny

Box Set Books 1-3

Box Set Books 4-6

Complete Collection Box Set

The Lawkeepers

~sweet romance suspense~

A multi-author series alternating between historical westerns and contemporary westerns featuring law enforcement heroes that span multiple agencies and generations. Join bestselling author Jenna Brandt and many others as they weave captivating, sweet and inspirational stories of romance and suspense between the lawkeepers — and the women who love them. The Lawkeepers is a world like no other; a world where lawkeepers and heroes are honored with unforgettable stories, characters, and love.

Jenna's Lawkeeper books:

Contemporary

Lawfully Adored-K-9

Lawfully Wedded-K-9

Lawfully Treasured-SWAT

Lawfully Dashing-Female Cop/Christmas

Lawfully Devoted-Billionaire Bodyguard/K-9

Lawfully Heroic-Military Police

Lawfully Contemporary Box Set

Billionaire Birthday Club

~sweet billionaire romance~

An exclusive resort—for the billionaire who appears to have everything but secretly wants more. After filling out a confidential survey, a curated celebration is waiting on the island to make their birthday wishes come true!

The Billionaire's Birthday Wish

The Billionaire's Birthday Surprise

The Billionaire's Birthday Gift

BBC Box Set

Billionaires of Manhattan Series

~sweet billionaire romance~

The billionaires that live in Manhattan and the women who love them. If you love epic dates, grand romantic gestures, and men in suits with hearts of gold, then these are books are perfect for you.

Waiting on the Billionaire

[Nanny for the Billionaire](#)

[Merging with the Billionaire](#)

(Entire series on Audiobook)

BOM Box Set

Second Chance Islands

~sweet billionaire romance~

What's better than billionaires on islands? How about billionaires finding second chances at life, love, and redemption while on one.

The Billionaire's Repeat

(Free with Newsletter sign-up)

[The Billionaire's Reunion](#)

[The Billionaire's Duty](#)

[The Billionaire's Christmas](#)

[SCI Box Set](#)

For more information about Jenna Brandt, signup for her [Newsletter](#) or visit her on any of her social media platforms:

www.JennaBrandt.com

www.facebook.com/JennaBrandtAuthor

[Jen's Reader Group](#)

www.instagram.com/jennabrandtauthor

www.youtube.com/@JennaBrandtAuthor

ACKNOWLEDGMENTS

My writing journey would not be possible without those who supported me. Since I can remember, writing is the only thing I love to do, and my deepest desire is to share my talent with others.

First and foremost, I am eternally grateful to Jesus, my lord and savior, who created me with this "writing bug" DNA.

In addition, many thanks go to:

My husband, Dustin, and three daughters, Katie, Julie, and Nikki, for loving me and supporting me during all my late-night writing marathons and coffee-infused mornings.

My mother, Connie, for being my first and most honest critic, now and always. As a little girl, sleeping under your desk during late-night deadlines for the local paper showed me what being a dedicated writer looked like.

My angels in heaven: my grandmother, who passed away in 2001; my infant son, Dylan, who was taken by SIDS six years ago; and my father, who left us four years ago.

To Ginny Sterling, my best writing buddy, my comrade-in-arms, my sounding board, my voices of reason, my partner in all things author. I love you so much!

To my ARC Angels and Beta Bells for taking the time to read my story and give valuable feedback.

And lastly, but so important, to my dedicated readers, who have shared their love of my books with others, helping to spread the words about my stories. Your devotion means a great deal.

ABOUT THE AUTHOR

Jennifer Branson loves writing historical westerns and filling her stories with mail order brides, cowboys, and lawmen.

Writing is her passion, but she also enjoys snuggling up with her hubby to watch old movies, introducing her daughters to the classics, and serving at her church.

She also writes contemporary romance as Jenna Brandt.

A NOTE FROM THE AUTHOR

I hope you have enjoyed Mail Order Misstep and plan to read my other historical romances.

Your opinion and support matters, so I would greatly appreciate you taking the time to leave a review. Without dedicated readers, a storyteller is lost. Thank you for investing in my stories. If you would like more info, please join my newsletter and get a 4 free stories just for signing up for my Newsletter.

JOIN MY MAILING LIST AND READER'S GROUPS

[Sign-up for my newsletter and get a FREE book and a FREE short story.](#)

[Join my Reader's Group, Jenna's Joyful Page Turners, and get access to exclusive content and contests.](#)

[Join my multi-author reader's group, Heroes and Hunks, for fun with some of your favorite sweet authors](#)

Made in the USA
Monee, IL
02 July 2025